MY PEN IS THE WING
OF A BIRD

MY PEN IS THE WING OF A BIRD

New Fiction by Afghan Women

With an Introduction by Lyse Doucet
and an Afterword by Lucy Hannah

MACLEHOSE PRESS
QUERCUS · LONDON

First published in Great Britain by

MacLehose Press
An imprint of Quercus Editions Limited
Carmelite House
50 Victoria Embankment
London EC4Y 0DZ

An Hachette UK company

ISBN (TPB) 978 1 52942 221 4
ISBN (Ebook) 978 1 52942 222 1

10 9 8

Designed and typeset in Cycles Eleven by CC Book Production
Printed and bound in Great Britain by Clays Ltd, Elcograf S.p.A.

"My pen is the wing of a bird;
it will tell you those thoughts we are not allowed to think,
those dreams we are not allowed to dream."

Batool Haidari, Untold author,
International Women's Day 2021

CONTENTS

INTRODUCTION

Lyse Doucet

"What do Afghan women want?" It's a question so many now ask, and so many now feel they can answer.

"Who speaks for Afghan women?"

Not a week goes by – sometimes not a day – without a Zoom call, a conference, a statement from somewhere by someone about the rights of Afghan women and girls that must be promoted, protected. And all these words have multiplied since the Taliban swept back into power in August 2021, imposing new rules and restrictions on the lives of women and girls.

Answers to these questions are arguments, analyses, a focus for activists. They're rallying cries on battlefields: nasty battles online, and the even uglier war on the ground in Afghanistan.

The Taliban accuse educated Afghan women of being a westernised elite, distant from the lives of the vast majority of the country's women. Others draw stark, stubborn lines between urban and rural experiences in one of the poorest countries in the world. Metropolitan women activists have responded, stressing their umbilical ties to their sisters in the provinces.

Now, this remarkable collection of stories offers us different kinds of words. They give us narratives that can start to provide more nuanced answers to these urgent questions. They do so because, like all great writing in this genre, they take us into the small but ever-so-significant minutiae of daily life. They do so because they are by Afghan women writing in the language in which they feel most at home – in Afghanistan's two principal languages, Dari and Pashto – impressively and painstakingly translated into English by Afghan women, and men, some of whom are writers themselves.

This book is more than just a literary project. It's a gift from the remarkable initiative of Untold: bringing Afghan women writers together, and allowing English-language readers to read their stories through translations that bring their words to life in another language. For most of these writers, even finding the space and peace of mind to write is a daily struggle. Literature is resilience, a release.

Inside the small, sometimes suffocating worlds they create, there are much bigger stories and disturbing issues – misogyny, patriarchy, terrible domestic abuse, horrifying oppression in both private and public spaces.

But this is first and foremost about storytelling, the art and joy of writing. It's what draws us in. We smell onions frying in kitchens. We hear the jingle of an ice cream cart. We hold a purple handbag. We sit on the "soft chocolate-covered seats" of a luxury car which could only be afforded by someone else. These are details we may easily recognise, in our own lives. We may also have eyed a pair of boots that seemed to call our name in a shop. We convince ourselves they fit. Of course they don't. What matters is that they make us feel so good.

But there is much we don't recognise and don't want to. These are the stories that cause us to recoil, in shock, in sadness. We shift our gaze from the page. I did, more than once.

A wedding is soaked in blood. Ordinary journeys between home and work are dangerous dances with fate. These are fictional accounts, not news reports. But it's literature drawn from real life, real loss. For much of their lives, many Afghans have left home, hugging tight those near and dear, not knowing if they will return in the evening.

We meet Hamed, a male teacher, on his way to work on the same route he has taken for eighteen years. The margin between life and death is breathtakingly tiny, counted in minutes. And there's a startling contrast between the reassuring rituals of hair and make-up in the life of Sanga, a state television presenter, and the rockets falling all around her. She just keeps reading the news.

These are chronicles about the day-to-day for Afghan women – and men, too. Cruel war doesn't discriminate by gender. Above all, these untold stories tell us about a society where men, and a web of societal rules and expectations, control so many aspects of so many women's lives, no matter their standing in society. And remember – they were written even before the Taliban returned to power. Afghan women will tell you: their fight didn't begin, and won't end, with the ultra-conservative Taliban fixing the limits of their lives in a deeply conservative society. But now, for many, it is much worse. The end of aerial bombing and ground raids by US-led NATO forces and Taliban attacks brought relief, especially in rural areas. But the battles at home go on.

We read how so much of life is lived inside – inside rooms; inside heads and hearts. In this interiority, characters reveal fantasies and fears, their dread and dreams. Women look into mirrors; they look inside themselves. They yearn for silence and space. They venture, like Zahra, "onto the balcony of her imagination, a queen". But even the mind isn't husband-proof: "Crazy woman," her husband taunts her, laughing, "come back to the real world."

Everyday places are crime scenes; kitchens can provide refuge but also pose risks. Knives and boiling oil are weaponised. Everyday objects possess outsized importance. Zahra dreams of buying a ruby red ring – to feel the "weight of the ring on her finger", to make the eyes of her husband's first wife "burn with envy".

There are turns of phrase to break your heart: "head hanging down as if she has been deprived of the right to raise it".

So many sentences will give you pause. So much so, I started searching – hoping – for happy endings, to feel good about Afghan women, about all women, about ourselves. They are there, too, even in the worst of times. You'll read of two girls' friendship, forged in the heady days of high school. This fictional account was inspired by the all-too-real and savage attack on the Sayed al-Shuhada high school in west Kabul in May 2021. Suicide bombers struck at a time and place designed to kill as many girls as possible from the minority Hazara community. I visited the school soon after the attack, braced to see and feel palpable sadness and aching loss. It was there. But so too was impressive courage and strength among its young female students, a generation of women ready to fight for their right to be educated, to have a future. It was unforgettable. So too, in this book, is the young girls' friendship, and an indomitable "spirit in the face of our struggles".

This is how one writer so wonderfully describes some of the people you'll meet in these pages: "a people full of joy and sadness and wishes and God".

To an extent, this book sets to rest the argument over "Afghan women". Of course there is no absolute uniformity; there are as many different lives as there are women. But in this collection, there are pressures and problems that transcend class, ethnicity and social standing.

The way a society treats women is often a measure of that society. There is possibly no greater example of this than

Afghanistan. Never have I worked in a country where the situation of women both dazzles and depresses. The heights of their achievements are awesome, the lows in their lives utterly shocking. Afghan women address the UN Security Council and top tables the world over in fluent English, their second or third language. But I've also met ambitious young women chained to their beds by their fathers for refusing to marry a man of his choice, or sent to prison for trying to escape abusive husbands – some even take refuge there.

For millions of Afghan women, it is a struggle just to get through the day.

This book reminds us that everyone has a story. Stories matter; so too the storytellers. Afghan women writers, informed and inspired by their own personal experiences, are best placed to bring us these powerful insights into the lives of Afghans and, most of all, the lives of women. Women's lives, in their own words – they matter.

I

COMPANION

Maryam Mahjoba

Translated from the Dari by Dr Zubair Popalzai

Nuria opens the fridge for a bottle of mineral water. Moments later, the water is boiling on the stove. She brews tea and sets a cup down, with a plate of dried berries and walnuts. Sitting with the tea, Nuria looks across at the photos on the wall.

In one picture, Arsalan is riding a bicycle and seems to be screaming. In another, her eldest son and daughter-in-law are holding Mahdi, three or four years old at the time. Nuria wasn't there when he was born or when he took his first steps. In the picture, they are all sitting on a sofa in California, a cake in front of them. They are smiling for the photographer, except for the child, who is looking at the cake. In another picture, Yusra is in traditional Afghan clothes, her green chador tied around her waist. Smiling, she is standing in the corridor, next to a vase that is taller than her.

Nuria gets up slowly and walks towards the TV. She removes the embroidered cloth draped over the set to keep off the dust, and presses the red button on the remote control. Seven members of Moby Media Group have been killed – the Taliban has taken responsibility for the attack. Images of the scene are broadcast, one after another. Nuria is saddened but at least nobody she knows has been wounded or killed. All of her children are abroad. Indeed, this is not a place to live. It is good they left, she thinks to herself. She feels satisfied: I did well to send them out.

She switches off the TV before she has to hear the statement from the Taliban. She puts the remote control down on the table and looks at the wall again. There is another picture, of herself with her sister and nephew. Nuria is wearing a short skirt and a loose blouse. Her legs are bare to the knee and her hair is short and wavy. Her sister's legs are also bare, but she is wearing a chador. Her nephew has brown hair and red cheeks and lips. His mouth is slightly open and he is staring at the photographer.

Nuria sips her tea. How old is this photo of us two? Thirty-five or forty years? How many years has it been since Dr Najib's government? She takes a breath and wraps her scarf tightly around her head. She looks at the clock, which shows it is ten in the morning.

She moves on to the next photo. It's Lailoma with three other women in Germany. Two of them have blonde hair and the other woman is Black and has dark hair. All three are wearing trousers. Lailoma is also wearing trousers. They took this photo in the classroom, laughing at the camera. Their mouths are open and their teeth exposed. What good dress sense Lailoma has! She is better dressed than the foreign women are. A slight smile appears on Nuria's lips.

The doorbell rings and takes Nuria out of her children's world. It has to be the cake and biscuits she ordered. She opens the door to the delivery man from the restaurant. He greets her, takes her money, and leaves. The sound of his motorcycle engine mixes with the hum of other vehicles on the road.

Next to the kitchen door is a desk and on it is a laptop that is permanently plugged in. Nuria uses the laptop only to chat on Skype. Each time she receives a call, she sits on the chair facing the laptop camera, constantly tightening her scarf. Each time she sits on that chair, she cries at the screen and kisses the air, saying, "I kiss you from afar, mother's flower, my dear, my darling, my precious."

It's Tahmina calling again. Her mother kisses her from afar again. Everything is fine at their end. The children are healthy and busy with school and sports; the men and women of the house are busy with their work and responsibilities. Only Arash, with a pounding heart, has a special story for his bibi jan. He sits in front of the camera and begins his sweet talk. He tells his grandmother that their neighbour, the lady who gave him chocolate and wore glasses, had been dead for several days and they only found out when a strange smell came from her house. Tahmina hurries to the camera to correct Arash. "She had not decomposed and she had not been dead for several days when they found her," she tells her mother. "The poor lady was ninety years old and sick. Everyone found out when she died."

Liza demands, "Food, Maadar." Tahmina kisses her mother from afar and disconnects the call. Nuria wanted to say, "Let me hear the sounds of your household, let me be in this corner of your room while you do your work and feed Liza and Arash. I will just sit here as if you are in one room and I am in another room." But it was not possible and she does not know why not.

She gets up and looks at the pictures again. In the hallway is a photo of Jahid and her, together. He had not gone yet. He had accompanied her to the studio to have this photograph taken to make her happy. On the day the photograph was taken, a strange sadness settled in Nuria's heart. God, what if Jahid goes abroad and leaves me alone, like all his brothers and sisters have? She had blinked while the photo was being taken, so the photographer had taken another. It was the second photograph that was framed.

And Jahid did leave.

What if I die alone and no one knows that I am dead? This thought brings a deeper sense of loneliness. She tightens the knot of her three-cornered scarf.

Nuria puts on her coat and leaves the house. There is a white dog standing at the entrance to the block. It is accustomed to hearing Nuria tell the guard, "Remove this dog from here so it doesn't enter the building." But today Nuria does not say anything. It is getting on for noon. Many women have come out to buy chillies and tomatoes to make salads for lunch. The shopkeepers are constantly sprinkling water on the vegetables they are selling, to make them look fresher and more appealing. The air is filled with the smell of mint and coriander and with the noise and motion of the crowd.

When Nuria buys vegetables from the shop, she feels like telling the shopkeeper, a young man: "Son, if I die – no, if you notice that I haven't come to buy vegetables for two days in a row – come and check on me to make sure I am alive." It seems a little funny to her, to say "make sure I am alive". What am I saying? She decides in her heart that she should leave the house every day for some reason, so that on the day she dies everyone will realise that Khala Nuria is missing and ask why they haven't seen her.

It is still only noon when she returns home. Into a small pot she empties the bag of lemons and peppers she has bought. She washes them. She dries her hands, rests her arm against the window and looks out at the mulberry tree, whose berries have ripened and fallen. What is left is memories of those sweet berries and their dark purple stains on the ground. The leaves will also fall soon, autumn is approaching. Another berry falls from the tree, unseen by Nuria. The height of her window and its distance from the tree in the street make it impossible for Nuria to see the mulberry fall. Taking a deep breath, she reties the knot of her triangular scarf and pulls a mirror out of her pocket. She glances at her eyes and cheeks, opens her mouth and sticks out her tongue. She whispers to herself, "I may die. What if I die? What if my body begins to smell? What should I do, God? What could Nuria have done to not die alone? God, if no one finds out, if nobody is informed, I will die a bad death. My poor body, my poor body."

A deep sorrow quietly occupies Nuria's heart. She opens the fridge, chooses an apple and puts it on a plate. She puts the plate on the laptop table and calls Hamzah, her eldest son. Hamzah does not answer, neither does Lailoma. She is also busy – she must be busy, that is why she does not answer. Nuria switches off the laptop and, still facing it, prays for them all.

The sound of sparrows filling the branches of the mulberry tree drifts in from the window.

When Nuria opens her eyes, her head is on the table. Her back is sore, stiff from sleeping in the chair. Her appetite is different that day. She feels like smoking, like in the days when she would steal her grandparents' cigarettes and experiment with them, rebelling against her mother. At this moment, she feels a desire strong enough for ten or twenty cigarettes; she feels she would like to light them together and inhale the smoke.

Nuria walks down the stairs and passes by the mulberry tree. When she enters the store, it is cold and empty, unlike the street. The white dog has followed her. Speaking slowly, Nuria looks at the salesman and asks for Pine cigarettes. He is a young boy. He hands Nuria a packet without any questions, he doesn't even ask if she wants a lighter.

Pine was the only brand Nuria knew and she wasn't even sure it still existed. But she thinks she has just bought Pine. She puts the packet in her pocket and holds it tightly so it can't fall out and someone won't ask if it is hers.

Nuria walks home. The white dog still follows her, but she says nothing. Back at home, she sits down by the window and opens it. She moves the chair closer to the open window so she can see out better. It's raining. She opens the pack, places one cigarette between her lips, and lights it with a match. She recites as she exhales: "Lailoma went to Germany, Tahmina is in London, Hamzah has been gone for twenty-six years. Jahid is also gone."

The rain slowly washes the leaves of the mulberry tree. The white dog is sitting just outside Nuria's door with its eyes closed. It's raining and Nuria is blowing out smoke.

DAUGHTER NUMBER EIGHT

Freshta Ghani

Translated from the Pashto by Zarghuna Kargar

It is late afternoon. The evening call to prayer is still to come. I am hungry, but I am fasting. My legs are weak, my hands are shaking. There is a kind of silence in the kitchen, but the sound of the pressure cooker, which has just started to boil, is breaking it, getting louder and more powerful. It has increased my fear too. I look at the clock: seventeen minutes past five. I turn the heat down under the meat. There is a big bunch of spinach waiting to be cleaned, cut and cooked for the guests. The kitchen is messy, and it is making me feel suffocated. I open the bunch of spinach, clean it leaf by leaf, and use the big knife to start cutting it up. Sometimes it is easy to take all my anger out on the vegetables, chopping vigorously. This is what I do. I haven't even finished cutting up the spinach before I start worrying about the rice; I have to soak some now so that it cooks better later.

Goodness me. I can't work properly today. I don't know the best way to do all this. I'm panicking. My heart is pounding uncontrollably. I have to get dinner ready quickly. I can smell the meat – it smells as though it's cooked enough. Oh, I so feel like eating it. When the fast breaks I will definitely be eating some meat. May God accept my fast and bless me with a son this time. What else would I ask for? It's lucky that I cooked the okra and eggplant last night. That makes my life easier now. Two dishes are ready. They will just need warming up later.

I can hear loud voices from the next room. My mother-in-law and sisters-in-law are laughing and talking loudly. What are they talking about, I wonder? God knows where Sharifa and Nazanin are. I am now eight months pregnant, and I haven't been for a single check-up. I feel that this one may be a son, but I am scared that something will happen to me. I hear a sweet voice. Who might this person be? It is my third daughter, Basmeena. She has got the salad plates ready for me. Oh, I love her tiny hands. She melts my heart with these little things she does to help me.

Cooking the spinach and meat is easy and quick. I finish making both. But how will I manage to lift the pot of rice on my own? I am feeling helpless, tired. Last time, when Auntie Makai was here, she saw me lifting a bucket of water and told me off. This pot is even bigger.

The mullah has now called for the evening prayer. Maybe someone will come out of that room and help me with this pot of rice. Before they do, I will break my fast. I haven't finished my first bite when my eldest sister-in-law comes in and says, "Well done you! The guests haven't even arrived yet and you have started licking the pot like a hungry cat!"

My first bite is now stuck in my throat. Fear prevents it from going down. I move the plate away – I don't feel like eating after this. I am standing quietly, saying nothing, though I have a lot to say. My mother always says not to be rude to my in-laws. She says you must endure everything. OK. My sister-in-law leaves the kitchen and my tears start flowing like a river.

I wash a big pot and put it on the stove. I increase the heat. My life is like the boiling water in this pot, happiness evaporating from it like the steam. My rice is soft now. I look out of the window, but there is no one who can help me to lift it down. Alright then. I will lift it. Nothing is going to happen to me.

As I lift it, I feel a sharp pain in my back. The water has started flowing between my legs. With difficulty I sieve the rice, add oil and spices, and put the pot back on a low heat on the stove. My legs have started to lose their strength and the pain in my back and stomach is increasing. I feel like screaming. I slide to the floor, in too much pain to carry on with my chores. Now the kitchen door opens, and my youngest brother-in-law, Hashmat, asks, "Is the food ready? The guests have arrived."

As he enters the kitchen he sees me. I hear him say,

"Sister-in-law, what has happened?" He splashes water over my face, looks at me carefully, then runs out of the kitchen. A few seconds later, my mother-in-law and eldest sister-in-law are standing over my head.

My mother in-law says, "You are a drama queen. A fake. If you weren't able to cook, you should have asked us to. If you die, what will I tell our relatives and the village?" My vision blurs. Hashmat gets angry with his mother and sisters, but I can't hear what they are saying. I feel like I might die. The last thing I remember is the black of the car seats.

Today is my third day in the hospital. I am breathing in the smells around me. One of my hands is connected to the drip. A white sheet is covering my body. A nurse comes in and scolds the women – those women in labour whose babies haven't yet arrived. If the women scream in pain, the nurses tell them off. There is pain in each woman's eyes. One is beside me, breastfeeding her newborn baby. I look at the baby and remember my own. I call the nurse and ask, "Where is my baby?"

The nurse, who is wearing pink lipstick, stands over my head. She takes out my file, looks at me very carefully, and leaves without saying anything. After half an hour she is back, and I ask her the same question again.

"Your baby is weak and is in an incubator," she says. "The doctors will tell you."

I say quickly: "Is it a boy or a girl?"

The nurse thinks for a second, then says, "I don't know. When the doctor comes, ask her."

My heart is beating fast. I really hope that this time I have given birth to a boy. God must have listened to my prayers this time, but, if it is a girl, what will I do? My life will be hell. My heart beats faster and harder. I wish for my prayers to come true. I really want a boy this time. God, help me; if this baby is a boy I will distribute gifts to the poor in your name. I will fast and visit shrines in your name.

I ask the lady beside me what the time is. It is eleven, and I still haven't seen my baby. There is no sign of the doctor. I look at my hand. It is all bruised. How could this have happened? Maybe I have had many injections in the past three days.

An older man and an older woman have entered the room. Perhaps they are hospital workers. No, they are not hospital staff. They have brought food to the woman next to me. There is noise from all the women, but she is screaming the loudest. She is eating at my brain.

The doctor has entered the room. She is very angry about the man, she is saying in a loud voice, "Haven't I told you not to let male visitors in here? Don't you understand?" The doctor is fuming. Her face is turning red with anger, and I am not sure how to ask her about my baby. I haven't even started talking when she leaves the room. Now she starts shouting at the woman who let the visitors in.

Oh, what should I do? There is a smell of kebab in the

room, and I am so hungry. Two more hospital workers have entered and they are distributing plates of rice, beans and a banana to all the patients. The woman beside me leans in and gives me a bite. I tell her that I don't want it, but she insists. I am hungry, but I am determined that nothing will pass down my throat. If this time I haven't given birth to a son, my life will be turned to poison. I am thinking deeply. I put the dishes to one side and fall asleep.

I wake to the cry of a baby. In the room, there is one baby that is particularly unsettled. The lady has two children – a one-year-old, maybe one and a half, and a newborn. It is the older baby that is crying. I tell her that she should have left the older one at home, and she says that they brought him in yesterday because he was even more unsettled when he was apart from her. I smile at her, and tell her: "God bless him."

The day has passed into night. I know nothing about my baby. I am not allowed to go anywhere other than the bathroom. The doctors are telling me to rest, but how can a mother rest when she's separated from her baby? What kind of justice is this?

In the morning a young doctor enters the room. She looks very fresh. She is wearing a light-blue scarf – she looks good. "Is the baby better today?" I ask her. "How is it? Is it a son or a daughter? The nurse says my baby is being kept in an incubator."

The doctor looks at me carefully and says: "Thank your God that your baby is alive. The baby was so weak that we thought it wouldn't keep breathing. What did you do that it came to this?"

I answer, "Doctor, my auntie said I should fast while pregnant. That maybe then I would give birth to a boy."

She is angry. "You fast and then the blame goes to the doctors? We are blamed for mothers who die in childbirth. How can these kinds of women stay alive? Who fasts during pregnancy?" She leaves the room. My heart is exploding: they need to tell me if I have a son or a daughter.

A few moments pass before a nurse comes in and announces that those mothers whose babies are in incubators will have them by the evening. My hands and legs start shaking. I ask the woman beside me for the time every few minutes. I am eager to see my baby. I am so, so anxious to see my baby.

It is mealtime again. I don't feel like eating. The lady next to me says, "Eat something. You will be breastfeeding your baby, you need your energy." I force myself to eat a few mouthfuls before the older lady comes in to collect the plates.

The day passes with us women chatting to each other. I didn't sleep at all the night before. It is my fifth day here. Finally, the doctors bring the baby to me and say I can leave. My eldest brother-in-law and his wife have come. They tell me to go with them, and I ask them quickly, "Is my baby a boy or not?"

They look down. No one says anything. I lose hope.

I take my baby and look under the blanket. My baby is a girl.

I walk slowly out of the hospital with my in-laws. My body is shaking. I don't know if it is the fear, or if it is cold outside. I look at my daughter and say to myself, What would have happened if you were a boy? I hope I die before we get home.

As we arrive, I hear singing and music. At first, I think the neighbours' son is getting married. No – the sound is coming from our house. Oh, good, I think. My brother-in-law is getting married. That will be a good distraction. Perhaps they won't tell me off for giving birth to another girl.

As I enter the yard, my youngest daughter runs towards me, her face unwashed. I hug her close to my chest, then clean her nose with the edge of my scarf. I ask her, "Marwa, what is happening at home?"

She says in her sweet young voice, "I don't know, Moor Jani. But everyone is wearing beautiful clothes. Look at my new yellow dress." I am anxious to learn what is happening.

When I enter the room, the women greet me by tossing the traditional chocolates and sweets over my head. I can't believe it. I can't believe they will welcome me like this, knowing that I have given birth to a girl. Everyone is congratulating me. I smile for the first time in many months. I say thank you. I haven't finished greeting everyone when one woman, standing on my left, says, "This is the first time I have seen a woman happy that her husband is taking a second wife."

It feels like someone has poured boiling water over me. My legs feel weak, my throat is full of pain, and my eyes have dried out. I sit down in the middle of the room and let my baby girl slip from my hands. A woman who is sitting near me catches her. The baby's cry is eating my brain. I hate to hear it. I don't even want to see my baby. I am silent, my mood transformed.

There is a lot of noise from the women. A few of them have gathered around me. I am still in my own world. Maiwand enters the room, and I run towards him and spit in his face. He slaps me hard across mine. I fall down on the floor, and he leaves the room.

Nargis' auntie tells her daughter Palwasha to give me a glass of warm milk, since I have just given birth. She helps me as I struggle to stand up. The kitchen is a mess, and there are dishes everywhere. Palwasha puts a pot of milk to warm on the stove, but leaves in a hurry as music and singing start up in the next room. The sound is making its way right into my brain. I get angrier and angrier.

The milk begins to foam.

I pour the full pot of boiling milk over my head. I fall to the floor. I am burning from head to toe.

Some women come into the kitchen. One of them runs towards me, lifts me up, and says with a sigh, "Poor woman. Her husband has married another woman."

Another woman, who has a big voice, says, "Poor woman. Her luck is bad. This is her eighth baby, and it's another girl."

DOGS ARE NOT TO BLAME

Masouma Kawsari

Translated from the Dari by Dr Zubair Popalzai

It looked worse when Saber was sitting down. His shadow on the wall seemed particularly lumpy. With his body curved over the paper, a person would think he was searching for something between the lines. He was thin and tall, but sitting like that made him look small, the curvature of his spine visible.

Saber was a petition writer. Getting this job had not been easy. He had no savings to open a garage. Carpenters were not doing well, and he couldn't afford to buy a sewing machine to work as a tailor. He had no connections, either, and didn't know anyone in the government offices. In the end, he concluded that there was no work for him anywhere in the city.

He had been very young when his father abandoned him and his mother. She had worked in people's houses when he was growing up. Now, in her old age, she was still doing the same job.

After years of searching for employment, Saber was able to rent a spot from the municipality on Sarak-e Mahkamah – the footpath that led to the courthouse. Some petition writers had their own sunshade; others, like Saber, sat under the canopies of the shops that lined the path.

A thin, weak-looking man approached and stood in front of Saber's desk.

"Do you write petitions?" the man asked.

Saber had wrapped his shawl tightly around him to protect himself from the wind and rain. Only his hands in their fingerless knitted gloves were visible.

Without looking up, he said, "Hello. Sure." He pulled out a form from the drawer of the small, old metal desk he worked at. The paper fluttered in the strong wind.

"Have you brought your tazkera, a passport photo and photocopies of your documents?"

The man reached quickly into his jacket pocket and pulled out a plastic bag. He placed it on the desk.

Numb from the biting cold, Saber's fingers could hardly close around the pen. "Give me your tazkera," he said.

The man hurriedly pulled the papers out of the plastic bag and handed Saber his ID card.

Resting a small stone on the papers to protect them from the wind, Saber nodded at the plastic chair in front of his desk.

The man sat down, looked around him, then turned his head and spat out the quid of tobacco he'd placed under his tongue. He wiped his mouth with the end of his sleeve and put his prayer beads in his pocket.

"Your name is Nazir?"

"Yes, it is."

"Son of Shir Khan?"

"Yes, sir! I have a fruit and vegetable stall in the market." Nazir pushed his head close to Saber's and dropped his voice to a whisper. "My father had two wives. When he died, my half-brothers did not give me my share of the inheritance."

Saber's pen was not working. He scribbled on the paper a few times, but it still wouldn't write. He secretly swore at the manufacturer of the pen, borrowed one from the petition writer next to him, and started filling in the form.

"Name. . .Nazir, son of Shir Khan. . .Permanent address. . . Current address . . ."

The man turned his head again and spat on the snow, the green of his saliva lighter than before.

"They said to me, 'You are not a son of our father and he did not mention your name or your mother's in his will.' I am now making an application for my rights as well as for my mother's. My father did not support us while he was alive. My mother worked in people's houses. We wore second-hand clothes and ate people's leftover food all our lives. I didn't go to school because we couldn't afford it. He didn't marry me to anyone."

"Why didn't you lodge an application to secure your rights and your mother's rights when your father was alive?" Saber said.

"Sir, I am illiterate, and my mother does not understand these things. Whenever I talked about it, she would say she had to protect her honour. She says people should not be given reason to gossip about my father. They would say she was badly raised because she did not stand by her husband and failed to endure the difficulties of married life."

"Do you have a witness if one is needed later?" Saber said.

Nazir got up from his seat. He adjusted his shalwar, wrapped his shawl around him and pushed his hand into his jacket pocket. He pulled out a small plastic bag of tobacco, took a pinch and placed it under his tongue. Shoving the bag back into his pocket, he retrieved his prayer beads and recited a quick prayer.

"Yes, sir! I have many witnesses." The quid in his mouth muffled the man's voice. "All the people in the area are my witnesses. They all know me. I can bring as many as necessary."

Saber completed the form. After haggling over the fee, Nazir took the document and left.

Nazir was Saber's first customer and it was already noon. The icy wind that swept up the streets and shook the awnings of the little shops hadn't let up. The pungent smell of the nearby toilets wafted into his face.

From the mosque on the road behind the court, the call

to prayer cut through the air. Some petition writers pulled plastic sheets over their desks and hurried off to pray.

Saber had long ceased to go to the mosque or pray. He had become uncertain of everything – even of God. He pulled a plastic cover over his desk, looked up at the grey sky, and went to the high concrete wall they'd built around the court a year ago, after a suicide bomb attack. The municipality had painted pictures of the old part of Kabul on it. One image was of Darul Aman Palace, which was rebuilt after the war. Another was of a girl giving a flower to an Afghan soldier. At the bottom of the wall were urine stains, some of them still wet.

Saber covered his nose and mouth and wrapped himself in his shawl. He untied the string of his shalwar and relieved himself, the drops of urine falling onto his shoes and the hem of his shalwar. The rising steam hit him in the face. He straightened up and watched the yellow liquid flow from the bottom of the wall towards the sewer that ran along the road, mixing with the melting snow and rain.

Saber retied the string, then bought a bolani from a nearby cart. He returned to his old metal desk, took the stuffed flat-bread from under his shawl and bit into it. Bits of leek caught between his teeth. He removed a thread from his shawl and flossed his teeth with it, swallowing the fragments of food it dislodged.

He was about to finish the food when he noticed the dog. The bitch was lying with her puppies in the hole leading to one of the toilets. Her pups were sucking on her teats. Her eyes were on him. Saber got up, threw the last bit of bolani to the animal, rubbed his greasy hands together, then wiped his mouth with a corner of his shawl before sitting down again.

He had noticed the bitch during the early days of his work at the courthouse. She would often sleep opposite him, and other petition writers would sometimes throw her a piece of bread too. The dog had disappeared for a while. When she returned, Saber realised that she was pregnant. Now that her pups were born, he would focus on the animal whenever he had no customers, or had nothing to do.

He took his quid tin out of his shirt pocket and knocked it against his palm several times. He looked at the right and left sides of his face in the small mirror attached to the back. His face looked thinner and paler than usual, his eyes sunken. Saber ran his fingers through his sparse beard. The hat his mother had woven for him completely hid his hair. His nose, now red from the cold, resembled an eagle's beak. He opened his mouth and examined his teeth, took a small portion of quid from the tin, and placed it under his tongue. The tobacco tasted bitter, but it was that bitterness he liked. It made him feel better.

Saber poured himself a cup of tea – the last left in his flask. The rising steam gave him a pleasurable feeling of warmth. It had got colder but it was no longer raining or snowing. He wrapped himself more tightly in his shawl and spat out the quid. The particles fell on the snow and immediately froze.

A passer-by stepped on them and they disappeared under his feet.

A woman in a blue burqa came and stood by Saber's desk. She looked along the footpath, her gaze pausing on each of the petition writers.

"Can I help you, Maader?" Saber asked.

"Salaam," she said.

Saber nodded in response. It was clear from the wrinkles around her eyes, which Saber could see through the netting of her burqa, that she was an older woman.

"I want you to write a petition for me. I have heard that yours are better than the others'."

Saber smiled and gestured at the chair. She sat on it, her plastic shoes buried in the slush, and immediately began to talk. She sounded tired. It was obvious that she'd had a hard life.

Her hands reminded Saber of his mother's, whose skin had become so thin from doing people's laundry that she needed to apply Vaseline to them every night.

The woman adjusted herself on the chair. "I was very young when I got married. My husband was killed in the conflict, leaving me alone with my six children. My elder brother-in-law, who has a wife and children, said to me, 'You will either marry me or I will take my brother's children from you.' I had to marry him for the sake of my children. His first wife did not allow him to support us. I worked and raised my children myself. My brother-in-law had a fight with a man over land. He killed that man. Now he wants to marry my daughter to his victim's brother as repayment." The woman sniffed then wiped her tears with a corner of her burqa.

"Should I write the petition on your behalf or on your daughter's?" Saber asked.

"No, no! On my behalf. If there is any problem in the future, I will deal with it. My daughter can't."

"Do you have power of attorney for your children?"

"No, what is that?"

"You should have secured it while their father was alive. To my knowledge, power of attorney goes to the paternal uncle or grandfather."

"I don't understand these things. All I know is that they are marrying off my daughter by force."

"The petition should reflect your daughter's own words," Saber explained. "Do you have any documents?"

The woman sniffed once more and pulled out some papers from a bag. At the top of the bag, which bore a picture of rice, she had sewn a large metal zip to make it more secure. From among the documents, she took out her ID card, her late husband's and her daughter's, along with a handful of photos that she placed on the desk.

Saber inspected the IDs one by one, then looked at the photos. "These photos are from a few years ago. You must take new ones."

The woman looked helpless. She picked up the photos and stared at them. "Can't you use these? It is difficult to get my daughter out of the house. They do not allow her to go out.

That is why she had to quit school. If they find out, I will be in trouble."

"No, it is not possible; these photos are of your daughter when she was a child."

The woman said nothing for a few minutes. Finally, she returned the documents to the bag.

"Take the photos and come back," Saber told her gently. "Then your job will be done. I will find you witnesses here. Just take some new photos of your daughter and yourself."

The woman stood up and walked away. Saber watched her disappear at the end of the road, her footprints quickly erased by the snow, which was now falling heavily.

Some petition writers had called it a day and left. The photography shop at the entrance of the street had closed earlier. On cold afternoons like these, the courthouse street was often empty and silence would prevail.

The puppies had drunk their fill. Now they were climbing over the bitch's neck and head. They would sometimes come to the opening of the hole and then retreat. The mother was lying casually on the dirt, looking out. A strong wind blew the pungent smell of the toilet, along with the odours of the sidewalk, into Saber's face. He was used to these smells; he was not bothered by them.

A group of girls from the training centre on the adjacent street passed by Saber's table. One of them bent down, picked up a handful of snow and threw it at the girl ahead of her. The sound of their laughter cut through the silence.

It reminded Saber of a girl he had once seen in the training centre when he was a student. He had spotted her only a few times and, because he was shy, he had not dared get any closer to her.

She was different from other girls and looked prettier when she laughed. Saber had taken a photo of her without her realising.

He had seen her entire family – almost! Sometimes he would follow her to her house, though always from a distance. He would walk or borrow his neighbour's son's bicycle to ride to her street. Once there, he would imagine the girl's photo on all the walls of the houses.

Then he found out that she had a fiancé abroad, and would one day travel to be with him forever.

"You're biting off more than you can chew, Saber," his mother had told him, but his heart was not ready for such talk.

Eventually he accepted his circumstances: that he was unemployed, had no home of his own, and that his mother worked in other people's houses. But he could not forget the girl, Meena.

The street was now deserted except for Saber and a few others spread out along the footpath. Saber lit a spliff and settled down to smoke. He put the spliff between his lips and took a deep draw. This was the only thing he really loved – his only real comfort. The smoke wafted through the air, multiplying Saber's pleasure. It no longer mattered to him that his father had abandoned him. He was not ashamed that his mother did the laundry in the neighbours' houses and that she would bring home their discarded clothes. He wished happiness for the girl he'd loved for a few days and admitted that he could not have made her happy. Now he longed for someone with whom he could talk – to tell them who Saber was, what he liked, what he wanted to do, where he wanted to go, and what he was capable of.

He was lost in these thoughts when the petition writer next to him shouted, "Saber, do you plan to stay here all night?"

He quickly came to his senses. "No, Kaka. I am leaving."

He got up and hurried towards the pavement. Almost everyone was gone, and the court staff were getting into shuttle buses at the courthouse gate. Saber cleared his desk. He had already put his cup and other things in the drawer. He locked it, and then, like all the other petitioners, he took his two chairs back to the market to rent out.

The snow was falling even more heavily when Saber returned to the courthouse footpath. He sat near the toilet hole and looked at the puppies. They were still little. He thought that they might die of cold and hunger overnight. He could not take them home – they did not have space and his mother would be angry. Nor did he have the money to get bread for them. He had earned just enough to buy food for that day, and to cover the next day's expenses.

He approached the bitch and gently petted her. The warmth of the dog's body was pleasant under his hands. She was breathing slowly, her ribcage moving up and down. Saber drew closer. How lonely was this dog? How did she manage with her puppies in this cold weather without food? What if they froze to death by the next morning? The dog must have felt his love because it remained calm under his touch.

He had never experienced love. His mother neglected him, especially if she was tired after work, or upset because of the landlord's behaviour. She blamed him for all their troubles. "If you had not been born, I would have remarried. Your cowardly father didn't do me any good."

Saber's teachers had shown him no love either. They pitied him because they knew he was poor and had no father. His classmates bullied him and called him Saber-e Kopak – Saber the Hunchback.

It was getting dark. A few houses had their lights on. Tonight, it was their turn to have electricity.

He thought of his mother. She would be home by now, waiting.

A cold wind was blowing along the street. Saber felt even happier. He imagined Meena, the girl he loved, smiling, dimples forming on both cheeks. Her hair – glimpsed from under her headscarf – was long and braided. Saber reached out to touch it. It was soft and delicate, like silk, and smelled sweet. He moved his lips closer to kiss it, but pulled back when he noticed that the bitch was following one of the puppies into the toilet hole. Embarrassed by his fantasies, he smiled.

Saber got up with difficulty and shook the snow off his clothes. He lowered his hat over his head, tightened his shawl around his body and left for home. Silence, darkness and the cold surrounded him.

Occasionally, the sound of a car playing loud music could be heard from a distance, then it would pass by at speed.

A COMMON LANGUAGE

Fatema Haidari

Translated from the Dari by Dr Zubair Popalzai

We were all sitting inside the translation bureau. It was a cold day and the doors had been left open to attract customers. It was so cold that our fingertips had turned red. Every time a customer came in with something to translate, we would curse them because it was so hard to type on a computer with frozen fingers.

We were already working when our boss arrived. Mr Soroush was a middle-aged man – forty-eight or forty-nine – who had diabetes and was injected with insulin every day. He was tall and had greying hair. He asked if we had eaten. It was one o'clock and we had not. My friend Ava, a quiet girl who only spoke when she absolutely had to, said in a trembling and frozen voice, "No, the beans are not cooked yet." Mr Soroush shouted at Javed, the handyman, and left.

Javed's job was to clean the tables and prepare lunch for

us. He was about twenty years old, had thick curly hair and couldn't read or write. Javed was always late and worked slowly. Perhaps the cold weather had affected him too, making him weak and frozen like us.

Finally, the food was ready. Ava, Naghmah and I grabbed small bowls of beans and a loaf of bread and went to the tiny, windowless room in the middle of the shop where we would eat and pray. The boss also used this room to meet his guests and friends. Naghmah seemed very happy that day, so much so that even Ava was surprised. She asked Naghmah how she came to be so happy despite all the work, the cold and the hunger.

"Remember I told you I spoke with Mr Soroush about my brother? To get some financial support to treat his addiction?"

Ava looked interested. "Yes, I remember."

"The boss wants to talk to me today. I think he's going to help me take my brother to the rehabilitation centre," Naghmah continued.

I found it hard to imagine that a man like Soroush would help, but I always hoped that even the worst human beings could show a little kindness.

I was thinking about this when Naghmah asked, "Did you girls hear that the Taliban are going to make peace with the government?"

I had heard these words too many times. "You believe it? I think you have forgotten that our neighbour's son was martyred in the war last year."

"I now believe everything. I'm sure that everything will be fine," Naghmah said, still happy that her brother might be rescued from his addiction.

I looked to Ava for her opinion, but she was quiet again. She wasn't eating, just using her spoon to play with the badly cooked beans. I think, in her happiness, Naghmah couldn't smell the burnt beans or feel the broken legs of the chairs we were sitting on. Our meal over, we went back to the outer room and started translating the documents again.

Soroush returned and sat next to me. He held out his hands, saying, "The weather is cold – let me warm your hands for you."

I knew he was not a god-fearing man, so I said, "Thank you. My hands are warm. If it's possible, bring a heater to the shop. That would be enough for us three girls and our colleague Mr Reyhani to warm our hands."

The other girls and Mr Reyhani agreed.

Mr Soroush was rich but illiterate. He didn't know how to use a computer or speak English – he knew nothing of the work we did. He laughed and complained that he didn't make enough money off us to justify buying a heater.

Then he went towards the other room, where we had just eaten, and called Naghmah. She jumped up like a rabbit, pulled her scarf over her head, and followed him. As she passed my desk she whispered, "See, I told you everything would be fine." She followed Mr Soroush into the room and closed the door.

A few minutes later, we heard Naghmah scream. We were horrified. We didn't know what had happened or what to do. Should we go into the room or wait? Our hands lay motionless on our keyboards, our eyes fixed on the door.

Naghmah came out of the room looking pale and panicked. Mr Soroush called after her, "You can take your money and not come here anymore."

As she was collecting her belongings, I asked Naghmah: "Why did you scream?" She looked very sad. "He wanted to touch me. I screamed and stopped him, so he is firing me," she said.

It was so upsetting – completely the opposite of what we'd hoped for when Naghmah went to meet Soroush. I signalled to Ava that we should support Naghmah so that she would not be fired. Ava hesitated. She looked at me and asked in a low, terrified voice, "So what should we do? What can we do? What if he fires us? How will we pay our university expenses?"

I told her that we would end up in a worse situation tomorrow if we let it go today. In the end she agreed. I could understand her reluctance: she was in a bad way financially. It was hard for students like us to find employment. But she agreed that Soroush had crossed a line this time.

We went to the boss and told him that if Naghmah went, we would all go with her. Soroush knew we were all poor and that this work meant a lot to us. He laughed. "You are welcome to go."

We went to his other office, across the road, planning to

collect our money and leave. We were owed half a month's earnings.

But Soroush had told his accountant not to pay us, and he told us to come back the next day. We didn't know what to do except go home.

My mother was surprised when she opened the door and saw me standing there, earlier than expected. "What happened? You are early today."

I did not know what to say and stood there debating with myself. I told her we had had no customers, so the boss had let us go home early.

My mother read my face and didn't ask any more questions. "I see. Welcome home," she said.

That night, I tried to think about what would happen. Where will I get the money for my travel and books? I asked myself. What will Naghmah do? What is she doing now?

Finally, the long night of thinking passed and it was morning. It was very early when Ava called me, asking me to join her and Naghmah and try again to collect our wages. I said goodbye as usual and left the house as if I were going to work.

It was a long journey, and the auto-rickshaw kept hitting the potholes in the road. The road was especially bad in the Monara area, where the vehicle jumped and jolted. My bones felt like they were fracturing from the shocks. Ava and Naghmah spoke of their worries on the way.

When we reached the accountant, he was again reluctant to pay us. He said he didn't have the money and that we should go to the boss. We thought they were kicking us back and forth to try to wear us down. But we went to Soroush again. When he saw us, he started threatening us. He said that if he didn't pay us there would be nothing we could do about it, since we were nothing but mere siah sar, helpless women. He was right: everyone saw us as prey.

The usually quiet and shy Ava said we must stand up for our rights. She told Soroush that, if necessary, we would scream and shout and show the world what kind of a man he was. I was angry and my hands were trembling like leaves. It was the first time I had fought a man on an issue, but Ava's courage inspired me. We stood firm so that Soroush wouldn't realise how scared we were.

Some customers came in and saw us making a commotion inside the bureau. They looked worried and hurried out again without submitting their documents, heading to another bureau instead. Soroush realised that if he continued this way, he would lose customers. So he paid us. But as we left, he laughed with the shopkeepers next door. "Harlots, eh! What are you going to do with them?"

My hands were still shaking with anger. When we got outside, Naghmah said, "You lost your jobs because of me."

To make her feel better, Ava said, "It could have been worse. We should thank God. Mr Saroush could have molested us and not paid us either."

I listened quietly to them.

The three of us walked towards the bus stop. I wondered what to tell my family. How would poor Naghmah afford to take her brother to the rehabilitation centre? But Ava's words had calmed me. I said to the girls: "God is great! We will find jobs again."

THE LATE SHIFT

Sharifa Pasun

Translated from the Pashto by Zarghuna Kargar

She opened the wardrobe, took out her skirt and suit jacket, and shut the doors. After getting dressed, she looked at herself in the three-piece mirror, brushed her hair, and looked again. She admired her reflection. Her long hair touched her shoulders and shone in the afternoon sun that came in through the window.

There was a pen on the dressing table that she put in her handbag. She looked at her watch. It was five in the afternoon. Hearing the car horn, she opened the window and looked down from her second-floor apartment. The grey car was waiting near the stairs of the building. The driver looked up and, seeing her, stopped pressing the horn. Sanga slung her handbag over her shoulder quickly and left the room. In the corridor, she called out, "Mother, I am going now. Bye! The car's here."

Her mother rushed into the corridor. Sleeves rolled up, she had a knife in her hand and tears in her eyes from the onion she had been cutting.

Sanga turned back. "Please look after Ghamai. I don't want him to hear me leave – he's riding his bike on the balcony."

She quickly went down the stairs. Her mother watched, praying for her daughter's safety until Sanga got in the car and shut the door.

Sanga reached the National Radio and TV headquarters, where she worked in the evenings. By day, she was a student at Kabul University.

She went straight to the make-up room on the left side of the building, at the end of the corridor on the first floor. The make-up lady, Maryam, was in the room. She was tall, with curly hair she had dyed brown. Her glasses were pushed to the top of her head and their string hung in a loop at the back of her neck. She was standing at the middle mirror, busy removing curlers from another newsreader's hair.

Sanga stood in front of the basin and washed her face with warm water, then, looking into the mirror, dried it with a paper napkin. Maryam asked the woman whose hair she was styling, "Should I do your make-up or do you want to do it yourself?"

"You will be busy with Sanga's hair now. There isn't much time – I will do my own make-up," the seven o'clock newsreader said.

Sanga sat down beside the seven o'clock newsreader and Maryam stood over her. She touched Sanga's soft hair and examined her outfit. "It is good you are wearing modest clothes."

Sanga didn't like this comment. She wanted to say that she always wore modest and suitable clothes, but at that moment there was a deafening rocket explosion and they all jumped. The seven o'clock newsreader whispered: "That sounded like it landed very close."

"God save us, I hope it is not the first of many attacks," Maryam said.

Sanga looked at Maryam. "If you do my make-up and hair quickly you will be able to go home soon. I will be here until late."

It was 1985. The opposition was busy fighting the Afghan army, firing rockets and targeting government buildings and institutions. People used to call them blind rockets because only one in a hundred would hit its target.

Sanga's heart was beating hard and fast. She hadn't kissed her two-year-old son goodbye, because when she did, Ghamai would cry and insist on going with her. She couldn't take him to work, so she usually left the house without letting him know.

Maryam spoke angrily now. "What kind of country is this? They can't let us live peacefully – how can we live and work in such a situation?"

It was twenty past six in the evening now. The telephone rang; it had a cord, as they all did in offices at that time. Maryam picked up and listened, nodding. She said to the seven o'clock newsreader, "They want you in the newsroom now. Hurry."

Then, too, radio and television were important institutions. This newsroom produced pieces about the leader, his cabinet ministers and their work, as well as reporting the victories of the army, which was fighting the opposition. At the end of the broadcast, there was some international news too. At that time, there was only one TV channel in the country that broadcast live news in Kabul city.

The newsreader quickly took her pen out of her handbag, looked at herself in the mirror again, put on another layer of red lipliner, and left in a hurry. As she closed the door, another rocket struck. Maryam was panicking. "This is definitely a continuous attack; more rockets will land."

Sanga was worried that Maryam might leave without finishing her make-up. The female newsreaders would always have their hair and make-up done before they appeared on TV. Maryam took the metal comb, divided Sanga's hair into sections, and curled each one. Then Sanga sat calmly underneath the hair-drying hood, which felt as if a warm breeze was blowing through her hair.

Soon enough, the seven o'clock newsreader opened the door of the make-up room and came in to get her handbag. She had finished her work and a car was waiting to take her home. Maryam said quickly, "I want to go with you. We live in the same direction."

*

Sanga was alone in the room. Looking out of the window, she saw that it was now dark. She didn't like being alone, so she made her way to the newsroom. At the top was the editor's desk. He usually stayed beyond his eight-hour shift. This was an important office and everyone from the editor to the reporters, producers and support staff, even, were paid for overtime.

As Sanga entered the newsroom, she greeted her colleagues and went straight over to the long desk in the middle of the room. One of her colleagues told her that not all her notes were ready yet, but she could have the ones that were. Sanga was busy marking the script and reading it aloud when there was another whistling sound, followed by a huge explosion. This time the rocket had hit the technology building, newly built, just behind the National Radio and TV headquarters. The explosion was so powerful that it shattered the windows of the newsroom. A sharp breeze blew in; it was still autumn but the weather was cold. Someone opened the door and said, "All of you go to the lower floor now! It's possible that more rockets will strike."

Everyone began panicking and left their seats. Most of the staff took their pens and papers with them as they hurried out, but Sanga left her notes behind on the table. Someone came close and whispered in her ear: "Don't be scared, everything will be fine."

Sanga said, "I have seen many rockets, they land every day. I am not scared of rockets, I am scared of God."

No sooner had she finished her sentence than another rocket landed, striking the front of the nearby administrative building. If you looked down from the newsroom window you could see the building's rooftop. As Sanga reached the door of the newsroom, a piece of shrapnel hit the chair she had been sitting on only a few seconds earlier.

Everyone had left by now. Sanga went quickly to the corridor, took a deep breath, and ran down the stairs, nearly falling. It was now five to eight and she had to go to the live studio.

Before she entered the studio, she took off her shoes and put on the special sandals that were kept in a metal cupboard. The people in charge of the studios didn't want anyone bringing in dust that could harm the equipment. Sanga had left her notes behind in the newsroom and was empty-handed. She went inside the studio, feeling the warmth of the lights as she sat down. The editor carried over the script and gave it to Sanga. It was time for the eight o'clock news. As Sanga picked up the script, she saw her face on the monitor in front of her and heard the signature tune of the news going live. She read the news bulletin, finishing on time. The studios were soundproof; no sound from explosions could enter from outside.

Sanga waited in front of the Radio and TV building in her make-up and styled hair. Other staff were also leaving the building in groups, big and small cars waiting to take them home. Everyone looked worried. Many workers were lowering their heads as they walked towards the cars, as if walking that way would save them from the rockets.

One of the drivers told Sanga to get in the car quickly. As soon as she was in, the driver sped towards the Third Macroyan, the residential blocks built by the Russians in the 1950s and '60s. Before the car had reached the first roundabout, a rocket landed in front of them. Sanga's heart started beating fast. She could hear the screams of men, women and children. There was panic and chaos all around. She promised herself that, if she reached home safely, this time she would quit the presenting job.

She had decided to quit a few times before, but each time that she had thought it over, she had concluded that a life without work would be hard. That thought seemed as bad as death to her.

As they approached the second roundabout, another rocket landed near them. It went past the car and landed on the edge of the roundabout. The driver and Sanga both ducked. Scared and panicking, the driver nearly lost control of the car. He stopped briefly, then set off again.

Now the car had entered her part of the Macroyan area. Along the way, they heard wounded people screaming and calling for help, but no one ran to help them.

At nine o'clock Sanga finally reached her home. She went quickly up to her apartment and knocked forcefully on the door, but it wasn't locked – her mother had been standing behind the door for some time, waiting for her return. As she opened the door for Sanga, her eyes welled with tears, which she tried to hold back.

Sanga went into her room, followed by her mother, and stood close to Ghamai's bed; he was fast asleep. She kissed him gently, touched his hair, then sat on her bed, taking a deep breath. Her mother now had a smile on her face. Sanga asked her, "Moor, was Ghamai scared by the rockets?"

"No, he was sleeping," her mother said. "He didn't even stir."

"I was worried that a rocket might have landed near our block."

As her mother listened carefully, Sanga told her that wherever she had gone today the rockets had followed her. "I had just got up off a chair and hadn't even reached the newsroom door when a rocket landed and its shrapnel hit that same chair. It was a matter of seconds. I got up and, when I looked back, the chair had been destroyed."

Her mother cried with fear, her voice echoing through the room. She went up to her daughter, hugged her, then kissed her. Sanga felt calm in her arms. Her mother wiped her tears with the edge of her scarf. She went out of the room and seconds later brought back a glass of lemon juice. As Sanga drank the juice, she felt her energy return. Her mother left the room, telling her to rest.

*

It was eleven o'clock; the dogs could be heard barking far away, the roads were busy with ambulances. The rockets couldn't be heard anymore. Sanga knew that the opposition had run out of rockets. They must be tired like her, she thought. She thought that they would be sleeping now and getting ready to launch fresh attacks the following day. But no one knew where the next attack would be and when it would happen.

Sanga held her head tightly between her hands. Her mind was full of news, loud explosions and ambulance sirens. She pulled the duvet over Ghamai so he wouldn't get cold.

She opened the wardrobe next to her bed and looked at her clothes before taking a few pieces out and hanging them on the door. She closed the curtains so the room couldn't be seen from outside, and turned on the TV. A song by Mahwash was playing. Before it ended, the power went out.

Sanga got up and drew back the curtains. Moonlight brightened the room. She switched off the TV in case the power came back on later, then lay down on her bed, but she couldn't sleep. Ghamai's beautiful face was shining in the moonlight; he looked like an angel child when he was asleep.

I saw Sanga the next day. She got out of the grey car in front of the National Radio and TV headquarters. She was wearing a khaki jacket with a black skirt, and carried a few books and her handbag. She adjusted her handbag on her shoulder, took off her sunglasses, and placed them on her head. Before entering the building, she looked around at the damage from the day before. She observed the scene carefully and calmly, then went inside.

THE MOST BEAUTIFUL LIPS IN THE WORLD

Elahe Hosseini

Translated from the Dari by Dr Negeen Kargar

A lady in white is watching you from far away. You stand and return her gaze – how much she resembles your mother! You walk through the carnage, the piles of fallen cement and pieces of metal. She is gone. Among the human flesh and blood, you see a wrist adorned with golden bracelets lying on the floor. The arm, severed at the elbow, full of blood, is shining from afar because of the bracelets.

You step on the velvet dress, stained with blood, pieces of flesh stuck to it. You step on the broken materials of the wedding hall as you look for your pot of espand. You cannot find it. You look everywhere for your espand, even in the dust and smoke of the explosion. You cough constantly. When you pass by where the bride and groom were standing, you step on flowers, which were neatly arranged just a short while ago. Now they lie in tatters under broken chairs and tables. You step on the colourful decorations that were hanging from the ceiling; now they lie, like the velvet dress, covered with flesh and blood, on the dusty floor.

Every dead person lying there was dressed up for the party – shiny, glittery dresses. You see a little girl with golden hair. She is lying like a doll, staring at a cloud through the hole in the ceiling above her. You want to kick her and make her angry. You hear the kids laughing at you, bullying you, telling you, "Muska has split lips," and you shout at them, "What is your problem? What do you want from me?" You see a little girl standing tall among them, telling you, "We can't understand you because of your lips. Why are they torn?"

You feel happy; you don't feel resentful; you don't bite your lips. You stand on a black loudspeaker and, one by one, pull the white tablecloths, stained red with blood, from the tables. You fly over them all. Then you go to the middle of the wedding hall and you spin, faster and faster, your skirt and the velvet flowers of your dress opening up. You spin and laugh and laugh. Again, you see the lady in white. You are happy to see your mother. But – is she angry at you? She looks outraged. Why is she not coming over to you? You want to go and hold her in your arms, to hug her tightly and be close to her, but she disappears again. To where does she disappear?

She stood on her right leg and spun the pot to raise the smoke from it. She took some coal and espand from the dirty bag on her shoulder and put it in the pot to make more smoke. She could remember her father's words with the burning of every rue seed. She said to herself, These are infidels. Their place is at the deepest part of hell. They have to die to rid the world of cruelty and depravity.

Her father's voice was getting louder and louder in the smoke of the rue. As he was tightening the vest on her body, he held her shivering little hands in his. He smiled at her and said, "My child, why you are worried? Your mother is waiting for you. I read this prayer to you – you will see your mother. You will go to paradise and meet her."

His words were running through her mind, and her blood was pumping faster and faster through her veins. She took off her shoes on the beautiful tiles of the wedding hall.

A lady was shouting from the middle of the hall, "Hey, where are you going?" Her voice vanished in the music and the noise of the wedding party. Muska took a white scarf, embroidered in red and black thread with an image of lips, and kissed it. It had a sentence written on it: *The most beautiful lips in the world*.

Her father was saying, "When you were little, your mother sewed this for you. She embroidered the image of your lips on it with her hands. This is your only keepsake from her."

She smelled the handkerchief and stared at the bride and groom as they danced.

Little girls and boys came close to her and taunted her: "Muska, the espand-burning girl, why are you limping?"

Everyone laughed and danced on to the music.

They danced around her. The little girl with the velvet dress and golden hair took Muska's hand, looked at her lips, and said, "You are wearing a beautiful dress! Is that from your mother?"

Muska wanted to spin her espand pot into the face of the little girl, but her hands were shaking. Someone told her to look at her trousers: "So baggy! It looks like you're wearing a dead person's skin." Someone called her Labshakari! Labshakari!

The little girl with golden hair opened her eyes wide as if in joy at having found another thing to say. "Smell her – she smells fresh. She has finally taken a shower. Today she smells good. She is clean." The girls came close and started sniffing her and laughing aloud.

One of them came up and hit her, before running away into the middle of the party. Muska's neck was moving strangely. She felt a burning sensation on her tongue, then spat a mouthful of saliva streaked with blood onto the white tiles of the wedding hall.

A lady with curly hair that covered half of her face walked carefully towards her in her high heels, then shouted to security, "Who let in this espand girl?" She repeated the question several times. Then, with sudden shock, she saw the white handkerchief wet with blood on the floor. She shouted, "Blood! Blood! May Allah curse you. Seeing blood on a wedding day brings bad luck." She ran after Muska to catch her, but . . .

*

Muska cleaned her mouth with her white handkerchief, closed her black eyes and found herself in her mother's arms. With a shout of Allahu Akbar! she threw herself towards where the bride and groom were standing. After the explosion, her hands and feet flew up into the air and returned to the floor of the wedding hall one by one, as pieces of flesh and blood.

Women ran madly; the blast caught them by surprise. They were used to suicide bombers, but not at a wedding. Tables and chairs were blown across the hall, as other guests stood still in terror.

The blast spared neither the women who sought refuge in the corners of the hall, nor those who hid under tables. It sent them from ground to air, air to ground, in a matter of seconds.

The ceiling collapsed into thick smoke.

You turn your head around the hall, from the entrance to the far end. You cannot see your mother among the wreckage – just broken chairs and tables lying on the corpses. The girls clap for you, and you dance again.

"We found your pot of rue!" says the little girl with the golden hair.

You get down from the table and join their circle. The women and girls you had seen lying on the ground, half-naked in colourful clothes ripped and stuck with flesh, drowning in blood, are now passing by you. The girls are following the crowd. The girl with the golden hair shouts, "Let's go."

You say to yourself, My mother! I have to find her! She was here.

They walk away and wave to you. You see your mother. She is standing just a few metres away. She does not laugh, does not smile at you. She does not talk. She just looks at you with disbelief, and her face glistens from a distance. Maybe it is wet with tears.

This story is a work of fiction, but draws on the real events of 18 August 2019, when a suicide bombing took place at the Dubai City wedding hall in Kabul.

II

I DON'T HAVE THE FLYING WINGS

Batool Haidari

Translated from the Dari by Parwana Fayyaz

The house is once again empty. I am here by myself, in an empty, lonely place. Whenever the house is empty, I feel a world of unknown desires crashing down upon me, head to toe. Every time the house is empty, I feel different. No, actually, I have always felt this in me. Not once, or at times, but all the time. I feel different. I mean: I am this different person. I want to be this different person. When the house is empty, I can be.

Today, in this lonely hour, in this empty house, I try to focus on my book. I run my eyes across the page and try to memorise it, line by line. It doesn't work, of course. I'm feeling too *free* to focus. Something tickles me, crawling across my body. I remember that the emptiness will last for more than half a day, and I smile, and the sensation grows. My breathing tightens and the grey walls turn colourful. The smell of the house changes too. It rises from somewhere at the edge of the front wall and spreads to the rest of the room. I want to close the windows, keep it in, but then I question myself: What about last time? When I ended up in the yard? I keep the windows open.

This time, avoiding the yard, I walk slowly down the little stone staircase that my father fixed last year. It leads to a century-old cellar. I feel my way down the stairs, running my hands against the walls. With every step, the stairs tremble and I take a deep breath. Nearing the ground, I can smell the old clay of the walls, and the sensation on my skin intensifies. I push open the old wooden gate at the foot of the staircase, and switch on the yellow bulb that hangs lifeless from the ceiling. It creates a strangely shadowy yet bright light in the darkness.

In one corner of the room are wooden trunks, lined up meticulously. In another, there are coffee-coloured bags filled with onions and potatoes. Everything is covered in dust. Walnut shells and onion skins swarm across the floor. I walk over to a pile of coal, small pieces and large pieces stacked on top of one another. The coal is so truly black that it projects an odd electricity. I approach the two large metal buckets used to carry the coals to the stove in winter. Behind these buckets is a wooden case, older than I am. My father says this case is called Hashdaar Khan. It is named for its enormous size and after a tradesman – Hashdaar Khan himself.

Hashdaar Khan traded in Baku in the USSR days, my father

had told me. Back then, cases like this were only made in the USSR. They made their way to Afghanistan via Ishaq-Abad with the arrival of the Red Army. That's how this case will have reached the markets in Kunduz, and from there the bazaars of Kabul, eventually to be given to my father's grandmother as a mahr by her husband-to-be.

The story goes that my father's grandfather lived in Salim Baig, a village set ablaze during one of those infamous wars. As a military man, he had to stay behind while the people of the village fled. He found the case inside a house and hid in it until no one was left in the village. Then, he dragged the case from one mountain to another and brought it to this house, to this spot, where it has remained. No one has ever suggested a new location for it.

I sit next to the case and try to open it. The iron plate of the lid is distorted, but with a little struggle I finally free it. Inside, the box looks deep. I smell tobacco and naphthalene: they fill the room immediately. My mother keeps our winter clothes inside this case. There's my father's woollen coat, the one he has worn during all the winters since my birth. She keeps my sister's and my jeans and leather boots in it, too, and a few folded bundles of pomegranate-red velvet. She adds the balls of naphthalene to scare away the moths.

There are some delicate Russian teacups in the case too, carefully secured in a cloth napkin. They are old, charcoal-coloured, painted with little flowers and birds, with a shiny white line around the lip. They were also a part of my father's grandmother's mahr. We only use them on the anniversary of her death. My mother makes black tea with cardamom for the mullah and my father. She pours the tea into the cups with care and asks me to serve it with fresh dates. We are strongly advised not to speak about such treasure to anyone. To keep Russian teacups with such care in a Soviet trunk can be a danger.

I lift up the teacups in their napkin package and place it carefully on the floor. From deeper inside the box, I remove two blue bundles, one by one, holding them firmly in both hands, and place them by my knees. Inside are my mother's wedding-day mirror, a pair of combs, and two little red-and-white boxes filled with kohl. My mother says these are the first gifts my father gave her. I admire her love; I admire her for keeping it safe in these bundles.

I place the mirror against the case and focus it on the roundness of my face. I pull the little stick from the kohl box and run it over my eyelids, turning them dark. Inside the box, there is also a lipstick with no lid, turquoise in colour around the edges, as if it were withering. I apply a little to my thin lips and then, with the tip of my finger, spread the colour around. I see my mother's wine-coloured beret with its soft loom-beading. I put it on. Then I put on her white shawl with its golden edges, which she has so neatly folded away. It spreads softly around my shoulders. The tickling feeling, which had waned a little, returns to my body. I look in the mirror and I am a beautiful young woman.

I clap my hands together, and then I start on one foot – leaping and circling. I dance, my hands resting on my waist. I stab the ground softly. I dance on the tip of my toes with grace and delicacy, just like any other girl. I feel as if all the boys are kneeling in a circle around me, clapping for me as I make the other girls jealous. Whenever I stamp my feet on the ground, the dust rises up into the faces of the smiling boys. And I feel shy. As I dance, I look upwards. I see the sky and I see the clouds in blue and white. The hem of the shawl touches my face and the sweat feels warmer around my body. I sense the sound of the tambur in my ears – the sound for which young fingers would give their lives. I dance as if I have been liberated from my body. Despite the heat of my skin, my liberty keeps me cool. I admire my own beauty. I open my thin lips, ready to sing out the poem that has always rested in my throat.

It is at this precise moment that I feel someone watching me. I turn around and my father shouts out my name. I pull the shawl from my head and toss it away. I feel heavy. The colours have gone; the smells are different. His eyes have turned red – bright red and smoky. He seems suddenly to have aged. He is pale, furious.

I dash past him and run without heed up the fragile stairs. As I reach the sixth step, he grabs my ankle and tries to pull me down. I struggle free and run on up, out into the yard and on to the exterior gate. I can hear my father: "If I catch you, I will cut you into pieces." My sister will be washing her face in preparation for evening prayer, I think, as the mullah starts calling. The azan sounds louder tonight. I pause in the narrow lane beyond our house, my chest heaving. I rest my right hand on my heart and try to calm down. I can hear my father again: "You bastard. When I catch you, I will give you a lesson for life."

I stand motionless but for my gasping. The soles of my feet are burning like coals. I take a deep breath and look behind me. In this narrow lane, there is little light. But there is enough that, when I look for my father, I know that he is not there.

I think back to the first time. My cousin was getting married, and my parents had begged me to go to the wedding and stand next to him during the ceremony as his only male cousin. I had said no, I didn't like the bustle of weddings, and I had to study for my exams. That last part had convinced them. But really I had wanted to stay home to feel the solitude that brought me comfort. They went without me.

I was left alone, and so was the empty house. I wanted to be seen; I was hidden from everyone else, but I wanted to be seen, myself for myself. I stood in front of the mirror in the hall and collected up my hair, which had grown down to my chin by then. I held it behind my ears and tied it with my sister's floral hairband. I pulled some strands from under the band, let them fall forwards and frame my face. My lips looked like blossom. I touched them gently, then picked up my sister's lip gloss from a table. As I looked up at the mirror again, I saw my father standing behind me, like a wild bull poised to attack.

I had no chance to speak or ask him why he had come back early from the wedding. The idea of running came to me only as I felt the pressure of his thick fingers on my wrist. He was gripping with all his strength. I couldn't feel my tongue when I saw his smoky red eyes.

He wrenched the band from my head and threw it at the mirror. He dragged me to the open yard, my legs walking me there against my will. I remember I did not see birds flying over our house as he dragged me into the yard. Normally, hundreds of birds, of hundreds of kinds, fill the sky over our yard. That day, though, they had seemed not to exist.

He kept hold of my wrist with one arm as he stretched his other back and pulled an iron dagger with a wooden handle from among a pile of rough bricks. He pushed me to the ground as tears filled my eyes. He locked me between his legs, his eyes by now completely red. Without saying a word, he made me understand: *be quiet*. He ran the dagger over and around my head and pulled away handfuls of my date-coloured hair. I remember the sound of the blade as it sliced through the strands, catching on them occasionally. When I stood up, I saw ringlets at my feet. I could feel clumps of hair sticking to the tears on my face.

I find myself crying again in the little lane. My hand is still resting on my chest. As it starts raining, I walk towards the mosque. When I enter, I want to feel at peace in this familiar place. But I am not properly dressed – not as I'd normally dress to come here.

Since that first time, my father has followed me wherever he can. He has started taking me to all-male gatherings. He thinks that by sitting among men I will behave like one, will become one. I cannot tell him – cannot tell him that I do not want to be like a man, that I do not want to be a man. So, I have picked a new style. Whenever we go to the mosque, I put on my finest clothes and apply enough oil to my hair that it shines under the bright lights. I wear perfume, so that when I walk in I am invited by the mullah to stand directly behind him during the prayer. From him, I get only admiration. The mullah admires my attendance, my cleanliness, my beauty. He shakes my right hand on occasion, but usually he just touches my hair. That's the only time I know I am beautiful. That's the only time I know I am admired, for who I am, for who I would like to be.

BAD LUCK

Atifa Mozaffari

Translated from the Dari by Dr Zubair Popalzai

Sharif had selected the freshest leeks early in the morning for Rahima to make bolani. This kept her busy. They reminded her of the days when her brother Ibrahim's wife used to come to their house, carrying leeks, after travelling the long distance from Azdhar to Zargaran. Her words one day were no different from her words the day before. She would say her piece and Rahima would listen.

"Rahima Jan, I know you are young and have hopes and dreams. But you have to accept that you have little chance of marrying – especially marrying a healthy young man."

Rahima had heard such words directly and indirectly many times before. But she could not stop wishing for a family of her own, to be a housewife, and to raise children.

Ali was her cousin. They looked after the sheep together, gathered firewood and fetched water from the spring. More importantly, they planned for their future. But times were unfaithful and did not move with Rahima's wishes.

When Rahima turned fifteen, she lost her sight. Her green eyes that looked only at Ali could no longer see him or anything else. She was overtaken by darkness. Rahima's parents could do nothing for their youngest daughter except take her to different mullahs and shrines. They made a pilgrimage and sacrificed their fattest sheep for the return of her sight, but the floaters in Rahima's eyes were bigger than their fattest sheep. Kabul could have offered a solution, but it was a long way away, amid killing and war.

Everyone was thinking about their own lives and leaving their lands and houses for the valleys. Rahima's pain was forgotten. Ali stopped talking to her about the number of sheep they planned to have; he didn't teach her about fishing; they no longer went to the spring together. Rahima realised she should stop dreaming of marrying him.

Ten years passed. The Taliban were gone, and Ali had packed up and left even before they had. He went to Iran, and Rahima, lost in darkness, remained. She wondered to herself many times if she'd still have honoured her love if the same had happened to him.

At twenty-five, Rahima had to open the gates of her heart again. Ibrahim's wife made this possible. She wanted Rahima to marry her brother, Sharif, who had lost a leg and an eye to a landmine.

By this time, Rahima felt she was a burden on her own

brother, although she had learned to use her hands and ears in place of her eyes. When cooking, she knew that the salt container was small and the sugar container was big. She knew that the knife always hung above the gas cooker and the potatoes were in a basket next to the stove. She could cook, do the laundry and sweep the house. She could go to the market from her brother's house, using a cane.

But she still felt like a burden. His only possessions were a milking cow and a piece of land on which nothing but potatoes could be grown. He had young children to feed and empty pockets. To have waited ten years for someone who left without explanation was enough. She had to make a decision.

Rahima wore a white chador and the mullah recited the marriage rituals. Someone who was a stranger to her until an hour ago had now become her husband and she couldn't imagine how he looked.

To provide for them, her husband Sharif sold vegetables on a small cart. He understood that he had to look after his family as able-bodied men did, even if it meant hours under a scorching sun, searching for shoppers to buy his vegetables. He didn't complain about Rahima's cooking. A year as his wife was long enough for Rahima to understand Sharif's temperament. She had grown accustomed to less salty food, strong tea and silence in the house. Her husband valued her, and the death of his previous wife was no longer a fresh wound for him.

Days passed normally for Rahima. She did all the chores

around the house, as she had when she lived with her brother. She knew how to sharpen her ears instead of using her eyes. She could tell when her husband was coming by listening for the wheels of his cart. She could tell the water was boiling from the sound of the kettle. She would pour green tea for him although they had never spoken more than a simple greeting to each other. She did not find the housework hard; to bake two breads and wash two pots and cups was easier than the work at her brother's house.

Rahima had cooked dinner and was listening to the radio in a corner when her old Nokia mobile rang. It was her brother. "Come to our place with your husband tomorrow. Ali has returned from Iran." She couldn't take in what her brother was saying. Her heart had started racing. It was as if a river had started flowing over a thirsty desert.

But the next day she remembered that she had a husband who had accepted her as she was. She prepared a breakfast of strong tea with sugar, and freshly baked bread. Even this held no appeal for her, though. She cleared the dishes, drew the cloth and left with her husband for her brother's house.

When they arrived, Rahima heard the women of the family talking about Ali's return. Rahima preferred to sit in the kitchen as usual, away from the gossip and rumours. She heard her sister-in-law telling her children not to be naughty. Rahima walked towards her voice and extended her arms to embrace her.

"Hello, dear sister."

"Hello, Rahima Jan. How are you? When did you come? I didn't notice."

"Just now. It's alright. You were busy with the children."

"Why didn't you stay in the hall?"

"I have no patience with the cheap talk of our womenfolk. I preferred to chat with you."

"You did well. Welcome!"

Rahima and her sister-in-law were still talking when they heard a man's voice. It was Ali greeting the men of the house in the next room. Rahima recognised his voice all too well, despite the years of separation. The men were all asking questions and Ali was answering them nonchalantly. He appeared to have no interest in answering their questions.

"So, Ali Jan, how is Iran?"

"It is good. The people live in safety. It is better than Afghanistan."

Ali seemed to be looking for an excuse to escape. Rahima heard him ask her brother: "Cousin, do you have a pill for a headache?"

"Yes, wait. Let me get one from Hakim's mother."

"No, don't bother. I will get it myself. Let me say hello to the women too and I will ask her for the pill."

Ali greeted the women, then Hakim's mother called to him from the kitchen: "Hello, Ali Jan. How are you? Welcome!"

"I am fine. How are you? How are your children?"

"Thank you, they are fine."

"I have a little headache. Do you have a pill for headaches?"

"It is in the fridge. Let me get it."

Ali, however, followed Hakim's mother into the kitchen. Rahima felt his gaze fall on her. She was sitting in a corner, cleaning the dishes. She had heard their footsteps but Hakim's mother said loudly to make sure: "Rahima Jan, look who is here! It is your cousin, Ali."

Rahima stood up and quietly said hello. Her sister-in-law was aware of their past. To break the silence, she asked, "So, Ali Jan, no wife and kids? Where are they?"

Ali paused. "I am not married yet." The voices of other women in the hall stopped Ali from continuing. "Rahima, Ali, Hakim's mother, what are you doing in the kitchen? We are starving." Ali had to take the pill and leave.

The men ate in their room, while the women ate in the hall. The women in the family ate eagerly, except for Rahima. Her appetite was also blind. She was asking herself questions. She felt as if time was moving slowly and this was the longest meal she had known. The voice of a woman praying at the end of the meal finally brought Rahima's wait to an end.

The dishes were cleared. Rahima made an excuse of carrying the tray of glasses. She wanted to talk to her sister-in-law about Ali. She held the tray in one hand, using the other to find the kitchen. She put down the tray and called to her sister-in-law. But it was Ali's voice that replied.

"Rahima, wait a minute. Take this money from me."

"Why? Have I asked you for money?"

"No . . ."

"But what?"

"It's your money, the money I saved for the treatment of your eyes. I asked all the doctors I met if your sight could be cured and they all said that it was possible."

Rahima did not hear anything else. Maybe she did not want to hear anything else. She felt neither happy nor sad.

"Thank you very much, cousin, but I am used to darkness now. There is no point anymore."

She gave the money back to Ali and left without saying goodbye. Her husband held her hand as they got into a taxi. She no longer wondered if Ali had been thinking about her all these years. She had to worry about what to cook for dinner and how to convince her husband to remove his artificial leg at night.

WHAT ARE FRIENDS FOR?

Sharifa Pasun

Translated from the Pashto by Dr Negeen Kargar

It was 1986. The war was raging across the country. The government launched air and ground attacks on the insurgents' positions, and the insurgents targeted government aircraft. They fired Luna and heavy rockets at government buildings, but few hit. Most landed on people's homes and local markets. More casualties were reported.

I looked at the hanging clock on the wall; it was quarter to seven. I dressed Saeed for school, then opened his lunch box and put some juice and biscuits in it. I told him to put on his shoes and wait for me in the corridor. As usual, there was no electricity, so I left the curtains open to let the light in. I made sure I had Halima's present, then took my keys from the drawer, locked the door, checked and rechecked that I had locked it properly.

Outside the estate, I heard the sound of a car horn. I

deliberately didn't look back, and it sounded again. It was Kazim, our landlord. It was the thirtieth of the month, and he wanted the rent. I held Saeed's hand tight and walked towards the car. When Kazim opened the window I was only a few feet from him, but still he shouted, "It will be twelve thousand afghani next month. Stay or leave, it is up to you." His bloated belly shifted sideways, full of food paid for with our rent.

I looked at my watch. It was five past seven and I had only twenty minutes to drop Saeed at kindergarten. If I went back to the apartment, I would miss the university transport. I asked Kazim if it could wait until tomorrow. The wrinkles on his forehead showed his frustration. "I need it now," he said.

Faheem's salary was hardly enough for our daily expenses, and we did not have any savings. "If we are leaving, we will tell you," I said, firmly. "Wait a minute," I added, after a pause. I knew that if I had said anything else, he would get out of his car and made even more noise.

Saeed cried and said he was tired as I hurried back to the flat. I calmed him down, took the money from the cupboard and counted out ten thousand afghanis, then put the remainder in my handbag in case I missed the bus. I could hear Kazim sounding his horn again. A neighbour shouted at him to stop hooting. "Mind your own business," Kazim yelled back at her. As we passed her flat, I apologised, gave Kazim the money and signed the papers.

I left Saeed in kindergarten and crossed the road to catch

the university bus, but it had already left. So I caught a taxi, and spent money that would have gone towards Saeed's juice and biscuits. I sat back and opened the window – at least today the weather was friendly. The sun's rays warmed the mountains in the distance and the soft morning breeze calmed me down. Thank god, I said to myself, that the sun is not someone's property, otherwise I'd have to pay rent for that as well.

The taxi arrived as some of the students were leaving for their lecture – maybe they were late too, like me. Others were walking around the yard, chatting to each other, and the rest were sitting on benches. On the way to my faculty, I saw Halima.

"Why weren't you on the bus?" She took my hand and led me to her office. I told her about the drama with Kazim and how our rent had increased.

"Can't Faheem ask the newspaper for a pay rise? That's what husbands are for."

"He is a dedicated government employee. He wouldn't dare."

"Like you," she laughed, "one of our most dedicated senior lecturers!"

She looked at my dress, which was black and white striped. "It's not for you," she said. "You are too slim, and it makes you look even thinner." Ever since our student days, Halima had been honest about my choice of clothes.

"I'll give it to someone," I told her. "But not to you!"

Halima's room was tiny. There was a desk and chair in one

corner, and a small coffee table with another chair in front of it. She took her thermos, poured some tea for both of us, and placed a small piece of cake on a plate. I wished her happy birthday and gave her my gift. It was a purple handbag; purple had always been her favourite colour. I watched as Halima swapped her old handbag for the new one. She twirled around with it on her shoulder.

"How does it look?" she asked.

"It's bright!"

"It's perfect," she smiled as the sunlight caught the bag's vibrant purple.

The tea and cake had given me back my energy. I stood up to go and prepare for my lesson, when a piercing noise, like the sound of metal dishes colliding and falling heavily to the ground, cut through the air. Halima shouted at me to get down. We threw ourselves to the floor as more rockets went over our heads and there were more explosions. It felt as though we were on the ground for longer than the few minutes it took for the rockets to stop.

"Alright?" Halima asked me.

"Yes, fine," I said.

This was our routine exchange after such attacks. She was always more resilient than me except for the time when she was taken to hospital and I had to give her my blood. I got up, went to the window and looked across the college campus. The yard was empty; the students had all run inside.

In my office, I tried to concentrate on a student's

dissertation, but, yet again, my eyes went to my watch. It was still only noon. All I could think about was our flat, and how one day we might be able to have our own house, far away from the likes of Kazim. I rearranged the books and papers on the tabletop, then stood up. Halima's arrival interrupted my thoughts, and she persuaded me to go for an early lunch.

A love song by Ahmad Zahir was playing in the large teachers' canteen, and the smell of dried coriander with fresh chilli was comforting. We found an empty table and sat face to face, as usual. The waiter brought rice and meatballs, along with a small bowl of salad and a yoghurt drink. I wasn't very hungry. Halima told me not to worry. Everything would be fine. She put a spoonful of rice in her mouth and told me to eat too.

At a nearby table, two of my male colleagues talked about the government housing allocation for lecturers.

I interrupted them. "Have people heard about their applications?"

"Yes, we received letters today. All those on the list have been asked to provide further information, such as photos and other documents."

Maybe, finally, some good news, I thought.

"You are so lucky, Halima, that you and your brother have houses."

"My older brother asked for land when he sent in his application, and he was also granted an apartment."

"How?"

"He knew a government official and asked for his help in the application process."

This reminded me of Kazim; maybe he also found it easy to get apartments from the government and was now charging us a high rent. Or maybe, like Halima's brother, he had had a few houses from the government and was charging a high rent on all of them.

"Does your brother live in the apartment?"

"No, he rents it out. If it was mine, you could have had it for free."

"You are too kind, Halima!"

"What are friends for?" she said, with a look in her eyes that I couldn't quite discern.

Halima lowered her voice. "My brother also got an apartment from the government in my name. He couldn't get it in his name as he already had two places."

I drank some water. "Do you rent that out too?"

"Yes. My second brother gets the rent for that one."

I put a spoonful of rice in my mouth and thought how, if only I had a relative who worked as a government official, he would have helped us. I couldn't think of anyone. Poor people have poor friends.

Later that afternoon, my lesson was cancelled, so I had a free hour and time to go to the director's office. As I arrived, Halima was coming out.

"What are you doing here?"

She brushed past me without saying anything. I had noticed

over the past year or so that Halima had stopped discussing anything work-related with me and chose instead to go to the director's office – from her first day, she had been attracted to him. He was a flirt; not a decent man.

"Halima!" I raised my voice and insisted she tell me.

She blushed.

"I went to talk about land eligibility and the application. The director added my name to the list."

"But you are not eligible."

"You were jealous of me and did not put my name on the list," Halima continued.

"The list is for lecturers who do not own a house or land. You already have an apartment. I couldn't lie."

"So, what are friends for?" Halima said.

The director called me in to his office before I had time to respond.

I asked him to show me the confirmation letter from the municipality and the list of applicants. He was distracted and didn't look at me when speaking. "The lecturers forget they have lessons. Each one has come to ask about the land application process." He picked up the list and ignored the first page, then turned to the second.

"Give me the list," I said.

He handed it to me. I looked again and again at the names but couldn't find mine. I looked one more time. Halima's name was there, but not mine.

"Can you see my name?" I asked him.

"Oh, I forgot to tell you that your name was removed," he said, nonchalantly.

"When?"

"When these lists were first created."

"That was a year ago," I said. "Who removed it?"

"I did."

"But I don't own a house." I was struggling to take in what he was saying.

"What do I know? I gave your slot to Halima. She proved to me that she was homeless."

I knew what that meant. It made me grit my teeth and my body heat up. I slammed the list down on the table.

"Why didn't you tell me? I would have explained my situation. Please do something so I can get some land and help my family."

"The list is with the municipality. No name can be added or removed."

The director's words made me squirm. I couldn't believe what I was hearing. I was in pain, but I wasn't ill. I had been betrayed, which was worse. I hurried back to my office.

I picked up the decorative stone from the top of the desk and passed it from one hand to the other. My confidante and friend, Halima, had turned my hopes into despair.

In the evening, I went to the kindergarten to pick up Saeed. He smiled and hugged me tightly. He wrapped his arms around my neck. I kissed his face. The exhaustion and agony of the day were forgotten for a moment in his little arms.

The next day, in my office, I had my head in a book but was struggling to concentrate. I wearily put a pen in the middle of the chapter to save the page, then closed it. I looked out into the corridor and saw Halima pass by, carrying some books. My heart ached from the dishonesty. I stared at her. We were like sisters. I'd given her my blood. I couldn't forgive myself.

I picked up the stone from my desk and threw it hard. It hit the wall. In the next room, the teachers panicked. Halima also came out. I turned away. Someone said a bomb had exploded, and someone else said it was the sound of a rocket.

D FOR DAUD

Anahita Gharib Nawaz

Translated from the Dari by Dr Zubair Popalzai

I am sitting in the hallway of the prosecutor's office. A police officer is standing next to me to make sure I do not run away. I have cuffs on my hands – the hands I used until a month ago to teach the alphabet and arithmetic to the children of the village. I had wished to see my hands covered in white chalk dust for the rest of my life. Well, life does not always go the way we want it to.

Three people were already waiting in the hallway for their trials when I got here. The second man, with a soldier standing beside him like a shadow, now comes back out of the courtroom, his eyes full of tears. His relatives circle him. A middle-aged woman – probably his mother – sits on the ground at his feet. She hits herself on her forehead, crying again and again, "Why did you kill her? Why? Why did you humiliate me in these final days of my life? You have left me alone, did I have anyone but you?"

I envy the young man. I wish I had someone who was upset for me today. My parents were my only hope, but to protect their reputation they would not spare me even five minutes of their time so that I could explain to them why I did what I did. This loneliness frightens me, but I must not be scared. I must think about Jamshid, who is lonelier than I am.

The third person in line enters the courtroom. At the same time, Jamshid and his sister appear at the end of the hallway among men and women in black, who must be relatives of his sister's husband. His sister's head is hanging down as if she has been deprived of the right to raise it. She is wearing a black shawl today. When I see her, I understand why women are called siah sar. She represents the true sense of the word: one who is destined for darkness.

At the age of nine, she lost her mother to torture by her father, a gambling philanderer. This was the same father who forcibly wed her to a lustful monster of a man, as old as her grandfather. Her brother is her only hope. She wants him to go to school, build a future and save himself and her from misery.

As she gets closer, I can tell from the way she is walking that her body is still in pain. After the incident, I have the same dream every night. In my dream, the girl's screams get louder and louder with every step her husband takes towards her. I see how he brutally pulls her hair and takes her to the corner of the room. I hear the sound of her husband's punches and kicks and, between each one, the girl's cries and moans. In my dream, I see Jamshid peering through the courtyard gate. He squeezes my hand and cries. I can see but I can do nothing. I am too cowardly to stand up to the head of the village.

In the dream world, I am ashamed of myself. I lean my head against the wall and close my eyes in shame, so that I will see nothing. Then I see Jamshid again. I see him running around the yard, looking for something on the ground. He stands over a basket of dishes, picks up something, and hurries into the room. This is the point at which I wake every night.

We have entered the courtroom. I stand in the dock. To my right is a judge reviewing my case with his colleagues. The court is not yet in session and people are leaving and entering freely. To my left are the victim's family, my lawyer and the victim's lawyer. I wish I could see some of my friends and family in the room, but, unfortunately, I do not. No one, except for Jamshid. Although he is no blood relation of mine, Jamshid feels like a son. He is sitting on a chair next to his sister, filled with stress and worry, just like the day he entered my class. He swings his small legs back and forth.

The day Jamshid entered my classroom, I didn't know anything about him. The school principal had told me that a new student from the adjacent village would be transferring to my class. When Jamshid entered, I guessed it was him.

I greeted him and said welcome, but he came in without a word. Keeping his head low, he went to the back of the classroom and sat in the furthest row. He was late: as he entered, the school bell rang for the last time. Dari language was the final lesson of the day. I asked for a volunteer to read the alphabet out loud and all hands went up except Jamshid's.

To include him I pointed my finger at him and asked him to recite the alphabet. He didn't move. I repeated myself, a second time and then a third. The other students murmured that Jamshid didn't know the alphabet. Looking at the other students, I said I would count to three and if Jamshid did know the alphabet, he would definitely stand up and recite it. Jamshid rose, his head still down.

I said, "Alright, let's see how much you know!"

After a long pause, he started: "A for Anar, B for Baba, Te for Tabar . . . D for . . ." but then he stopped. The rest of the students were quietly nudging him, "Daud, Daud," but it was as though he couldn't hear them. I did not want him to sit. I asked him to start over. He started again: "A for Anar, B for Baba, Te for Tabar . . . D for . . ." and then there was silence.

I noticed that both his hands had started to tremble. I walked over to him. His whole body was shaking. I could not understand what had made this poor child hurt so much. I put my hand on his back and said, "No problem, try to learn the alphabet well before our next Dari session."

I went back to the front of the class. The period finished and the school bell rang. Eagerly, the students left the classroom.

I watched Jamshid, who did not move until the last pupil had left the class. Then, he quietly gathered his books and got up from behind his desk. I needed to hear at least one word from him. He passed my desk, eager to leave, but I stopped him and tried to make him look me in the eye. I took his hands and assured him that if there was a problem, I would help him solve it. I promised him that I would teach him the alphabet myself.

After a short pause, he broke down. Tears were flowing from his eyes as he said, "Leila, Leila." I realised he was not in a state to explain his problem to me. I hugged him and said I would help him solve all his problems. I wiped his tears and told him to return home. "We will talk tomorrow," I said. Jamshid walked slowly out of the classroom.

After speaking to several villagers, I learned that he had transferred to our school because his sister had married the chief of our village. Since Jamshid had a stepmother and his father was a gambler and a philanderer, his sister would not accept the marriage unless her brother also came to her husband's house and lived there with her. In the end, the girl's father and her husband agreed to her request and seven-year-old Jamshid ended up in Year One in our village.

I began spending an hour a day with him, when we would chat together. It brought us very close. Gradually he changed in class, too. When he entered the room, he would smile at me, then greet his classmates energetically.

*

But one day – that day – he entered the classroom silently, hanging his head again. I called his name and asked him why he was late, but he went straight to his chair without saying a word.

I told him to recite the alphabet as punishment for coming in late. But he didn't say anything; he remained seated with his head down. When I asked him in a more serious voice to get up, he slowly stood, still staring at the ground.

The catch in his voice made me feel as if all the sorrows of the world had accumulated in his throat. Just like the first day, his voice faded when he reached the letter D. He tried to say "D for Daud" a second time, but only "D" could be heard. I noticed that his hands were shaking. He raised his head and stared into my eyes as if the lump in his throat was about to explode. After a short pause, he ran to the door and hurried out of the classroom.

There was no peace left in me. I could not ignore him and continue teaching. I told the students that something urgent had come up and that I had to leave for a few minutes. I asked them to stay in the classroom and review their lessons until I returned. I rushed to the school gate to find Jamshid. From the school grounds, I saw him running past the hill, towards his sister's house.

I followed him to the house of the village chief. Jamshid was sitting by the garden wall, crying softly and occasionally peeking into the house. When I approached him, he immediately got up. He didn't say anything – just pointed to the house.

I didn't understand. He took my hand and slowly led me to the gate. He pointed to the curtained window of a room. I could hear sounds from behind the curtain: the sound of beating, followed by a woman's crying and screaming.

We saw the shadow of a person grab a woman by the hair and drag her to the corner of the room. The woman was screaming so hard that even a rock would melt. Then, for a moment, it was silent. The woman's voice disappeared and a man could be heard panting.

When the woman's voice went quiet, I realised that Jamshid's mind was elsewhere. He let go of my hand and ran into the garden, like someone who has lost something. He wandered around in bewilderment. He ran to the basket of dishes in the middle of the yard. He picked something up and hurried into the room. I quickly followed him.

I saw the little girl lying on the floor with the chief on top of her, strangling her.

I was panicking but Jamshid took the initiative. He attacked the chief from behind with the knife that he had picked up. Without hesitation, he furiously stabbed him in the back again and again. I could see he was letting out all his rage. Although I could have, I did not stop him. The man deserved worse than that. I counted the number of times Jamshid stabbed the chief in the back. One, two . . . eleven. When he struck for the twelfth time we heard the bodyguards approaching.

Jamshid threw down the knife and looked for a way to escape. He was panicking. My mind was not in the right place either. I hugged Jamshid and whispered in his ear, "I will fix everything. You must run away. Wash your hands and change your clothes." As he shuddered and tears welled up in his eyes, I continued slowly, "Be sure to read your lessons and save yourself and your sister from this misery." I kissed him on the head and pushed him towards the door. Jamshid jumped through the window and fled. I picked the knife up from the floor and went over to the chief's body. As his bodyguards entered, I stabbed him in the back for the thirteenth time.

The court is now in session and the judge begins to ask his questions. I answer casually. The last question is, "Mr —, do you admit that you killed Daud Khan by stabbing him with a knife thirteen times while you were fully aware and of sound mind?"

Jamshid raises his head and stares into my eyes with a hopeful look. His look makes me more steadfast. I smile at him, turn my face to the judge and say, "Yes. I admit that I killed Daud Khan with a knife by stabbing him thirteen times while I was of sound mind. I admit it, Judge."

I look at Jamshid and see that he's stopped anxiously swinging his legs. He is holding his head high and he looks at me with eyes that shout joy. By lifting this crime off his shoulders, I have made him as light as a feather in the air. Although the judge sentences me to life imprisonment, I do not feel any sadness in my heart.

The trial is officially over. Everyone leaves, one by one.

Jamshid's sister also leaves, followed by Jamshid. He smiles at me as he walks past. As he walks, he begins to recite the alphabet quietly. When he reaches the letter D he looks back at me from the courtroom door and continues loudly until he gets to the end.

FALLING FROM THE SUMMIT OF DREAMS

Parand

Translated from the Dari by Parwana Fayyaz

It is mid-October. The trees shimmer with the fruits they have nurtured through the storms of spring and summer. The autumn has come with its blessings, gifting and granting. The people do their share, collecting the harvest in bags and boxes. Zahra, too, is becoming busier in the garden – her garden – day by day.

As she opens the gate at the back of the garden, its broken iron edges bite at her scarf and skirt. She pulls herself through, carrying her one torn plastic shoe in her hand. Something tied in a knot in a corner of her scarf swings like a pendulum, left to right to left.

What a life, she says to herself. I marry to be freed from the burden of poverty, and my condition only worsens. My husband's old wife, Roshan Gul – her fortune is bright and mine is dark. They are right, those who say, "Happy is the bride that the sun shines on." They are right when they say, "When fortune eats, the face cries."

She twirls the torn shoe angrily above her head, then tosses it as far as her strength allows. She feels her misery fly into the air.

She begins walking. Her feet are bare but her heart is lighter.

"Patience is bitter, but its fruit is sweet," she mutters. "The day will come when I will buy a ruby ring from the gold-smith in the village, and wear it until Roshan Gul's eyes burn with envy. She is only arrogant because of that ring, and she only has it because she inherited it from her mother." Zahra remembers her own mother, who, like all women, wanted such a ring. She never got one, so she never had one to pass on.

As she says these words, she touches the knot in her scarf as if something sacred is bundled there. She smiles a smile of victory, of indestructible happiness.

Just a few more days, a few more almonds, and I'll have the money for the ring.

She closes her eyes and imagines the weight of it on her finger. She holds her rough hand out, covered in cuts from gardening, and pictures the ruby ring shining red.

It has a warmth. She's in the heart of the winter sun. It heats her body. Its purity takes her away from the reality she wants not to be part of. She walks onto the balcony of her imagination, a queen. She wears a green velvet dress with innumerable pleats, sewn by ten seamstresses from the village. Her hands are soft and young, and on one finger is the ruby ring, the stone set in gold plate. She worries suddenly that she might have come here wearing her old plastic shoes. She trembles with dread. What if Roshan Gul, who is standing at a distance, envious like the rest of the women, sees her in those shoes? She peeks down at her feet, relieved to see golden slippers like those she had once seen on the richest woman in the village, and at which she had sighed with covetous grief.

She suddenly feels a sharp pain at her waist. Too much standing, she thinks to herself. I should go and rest while the other women stand and wait for me. But the mischievous laughter of her stepson drags her back to bitter reality, and she sees the stone he has thrown at her.

"Crazy woman," he says. "Are you roaming in your dream world again? Talking to yourself? Ha, how long have you been there? Come back to the real world," he taunts, laughing.

She sends him away and tries to go back to her daydreaming. But the hellish voice of the boy has ruined her joy. Sami Jan is his father's son – he kills birds, ties butterflies and bees up with string. And now that Zahra has married his father, Sami Jan has found another cruel new pastime.

Zahra starts walking and, after a while, reaches a half-collapsed building. She pushes open its heavy wooden gate and enters. There's not a soul in its yard. She walks towards a barn filled with bales of straw. After some searching amid the piles, she is relieved to find the bag of almonds. She opens the knot in the corner of her chador and pours the almonds into the bag. She feels its weight, then returns it to its hiding place. She has been collecting these special soft-shell almonds that only her husband is allowed to eat in the winter.

Almost there, almost there. A few more knots in my scarf and soon I'll be able to buy that ring.

A sudden feeling of being watched makes her uneasy. Through a vent in the barn she senses a pair of eyes. She stands up straight and searches for their owner, but nothing. A common delusion, she thinks, for people who do secret things.

She walks home. As she enters the house, she runs into Roshan Gul. She turns around to avoid her gaze.

"What were you doing in the garden for so long?" Roshan Gul says. "Were you daydreaming about a new lover? Hurry up and start cooking the dinner. Haji Jan will kill you if it's late."

Zahra has learned to ignore Roshan Gul. With an attempt at dignity, she leaves the room.

In the kitchen, which has become her refuge, she pours oil into a pan. A few minutes into heating it, she hears the loud noise of something falling. Her heart sinks. Fear grips her body. The sound, she is sure, is of an almond bag falling to the ground. He has found it; her secret is exposed. She doesn't dare to raise her head and look at the bag, her dreams slumped on the floor.

No, she is determined not to look. She will just accept the beatings and the punishment that will result.

But no one says anything, so she eventually lifts her head and turns around. There is just the pile of firewood that her stepson had collected earlier. She laughs quietly to herself, thinking, I am so scared, and for nothing. I am my own enemy. I should just relax.

She washes away her worries and busies herself making dinner. She slices onions and throws them into the hot oil. Time passes as she washes, cuts, boils, cooks. And then someone gives her hair a strong pull and pushes her onto the ground. Her husband.

Zahra screams with pain.

"What is wrong with you?" she shouts.

"What is wrong with me? Ha!" she hears her husband say.

With a smirk he calls for his son to bring over the bag of almonds. He drags it next to her and pours the nuts on the ground.

"What do you have to say about these?" He pulls her hair violently. He slaps her across the face. The force of his hand makes her ears ring with a hundred bees feasting on her brain. "I want an answer!" he screams.

Roshan Gul appears, smiling. "Are you deaf? Haji wants an answer."

"An answer! For what?" She repeatedly tries to get up from the ground, but her husband kicks her hard in her side. She gives in. "I want a ring – a ruby ring from the goldsmith, the same kind of ring that Roshan Gul has."

Father, wife and son laugh loudly in chorus. Her husband

grabs her neck, and tightens his grip until she begins to choke.

"She desires a ring! Ha. And from the same goldsmith in our village! Ha."

Roshan Gul encourages him to press her neck harder.

"Don't laugh at me," Zahra implores, struggling to breathe. "My desire is not wrong."

When the boy realises that Zahra is on the way to being choked to death, he interrupts. "Be careful, Aba, or you might kill her. And then you will have to go to prison. There are other ways to punish a thief." Heir to this violence, he looks at his father and, without saying a word, they come to an agreement. Zahra's husband loosens his grip. Coughing, she pulls herself towards the door in the hope of getting away. But there is no hope. Roshan Gul and Sami Jan grab her and pass her into her husband's clutches. He pulls her hand towards the burning oil.

"What point will there be in your desires now?" he says.

AN IMPRINT ON THE WALL

Masouma Kawsari

Translated from the Dari by Parwana Fayyaz

Ranna was standing behind the two concrete barrier walls when the explosion took place – the one that had thrown everything up into the sky. On the way back down to earth, half her body had come to rest between the two walls, which ran parallel only a metre apart from each other. That was where she'd returned – or half of her at least. The other half never came back down from the sky. Maybe it did, and was collected by the ambulance, or maybe the water of the Kabul River swept it away. But the half that did come back down was lying still between the walls.

Her face was covered in blood and her eyes had been turned red by it – or maybe by staring at the blood around her. From Ranna's viewpoint, one of the walls looked as if it had been covered in a great red veil. As the blood ran, and dried, and paused, it made lines in that great veil. And though Ranna's eyes were still, it seemed that the lines were moving. They formed a shape – an imprint of a short, fat man, the manager of the architect's firm where Ranna worked. If he had seen Ranna absent from work like this, he'd have docked her pay. Her co-workers used to say, "The manager has no education and resents it, and that's why he treats everyone so terribly. His wife is related to the wife of the company president, and when the new president was appointed, he asked the manager to join him."

Ranna pictured the face of the president in the lines on the wall. A shaved face with no turban atop it. But if the lines ran to form a long beard from his stubble, and if others made a turban on his head, he would look just like her father. She had seen photos of him from years ago, standing with men in their perahan tunban, their trousers rolled up. With their turbans and well-cut beards, they stood leaning against their Kalashnikovs, or with a rocket resting on their shoulders. Amid the rocks and trees, they stood smiling.

When she had first seen those photos, her mother had explained to her, "When you turned four, there was a revolution. Your father smuggled us into Iran, and then he returned to the country for jihad." He had sent a few photos in his first year back in Afghanistan, her mother said. But mostly they heard about him through rumours: sometimes, people brought the news that he had become a mujahid; others said he had married another woman and had children with her. A few years later, no one brought any news from him. Now she thought about her mother, suffering with her Alzheimer's, and worried: what would become of her?

She stopped thinking about her parents, because there were voices coming from the walls: officials, who worked for the manager, were introducing her colleague Amir. The officials were all a little slimmer and taller than the manager, and Amir was slimmer and taller still. The lines on the wall moved accordingly. Ranna's colleagues used to say, "When the manager first came, he seemed tall. But after a few years he became fatter. Then he bought a car, married for good, sent his parents on pilgrimage to Hajj and two of his brothers abroad." A short, fat imprint on the wall.

Another voice joined the echoes between the two walls: Takbeer, who had been absent for three days. The manager had reduced his pay. There was another echo – the sound of the explosion that had silenced them. And then the voice of her father. "My wife could not give me a son, so I married for a second time. I just could not leave my inheritance to my daughter." And then the sound of the ambulance that had arrived to wash the streets.

Half of her body, her purse, her mother's memories, her father's photographs – the water had washed them all away.

Her eyes were still, open wide, her pupils big. Her arms had fallen to her sides; they had lost all feeling and were lying motionless. The blood had spattered on the ground between two walls, clotted, and was slowly drying. The flies were congregating, their eggs slowly transforming into larvae. The little larvae, dressed in white, crawled around one another. A line of yellow ants was busy cutting and eating. The task of decomposition had started.

Two parallel lines of blood on the wall had turned perpendicular as they dried with time, becoming the lines of a crossroad.

That day, on the side of the street, she said her goodbyes to everyone.

Ranna had chosen her path a long time ago: that if she did not succeed in the Kankor examination, she would not accept a path in life that would take her to a place where she would feel foreign. She had made her decision while she was still in Iran, long after her father was taken captive by the communists for his beliefs. She was living with her family in Mashhad, where, by then, they had been for years.

One day, after school, as she was sweating under her black chador, feeling weary, her friend said that she was tired of the place and wanted to leave. Ranna had agreed. "I would like to go, too – to find my father, my forebears, my identity."

Her friend had laughed at her and said, "I am going to Germany to find myself an identity. I am tired of this chador, of this hijab, of everything here. I want to build everything anew."

"I wish to go to Kabul," Ranna had said. "My father is alive. He is not Taliban anymore – he's in Parliament. He's the people's representative. I will find him. And I am sure that my wounds of loneliness will heal."

In time, she did find him – when she returned to Afghanistan at twenty-one, a year before she started her studies in architecture. His appearance had changed. The white hairs of age could not be hidden by him shaving his beard and moustache, and she doubted if she had ever seen her father in a white shirt, suit and tie, the way he was dressed that day. She had asked him, "Do you have a daughter with the name Ranna?" But he had changed only in appearance, not in belief. He was silent, and the memory of his words ran through her head: "I just could not leave my inheritance to my daughter."

She left him and went to Sangcharak, to the village she had left seventeen years before. She found that almost everything had fallen to the ground: the graves of the nameless remained intact, but the houses, the streets and the gardens were now dust and stones.

In Mashhad, in her first few years of wearing a scarf, Thirty Metres Street on which they lived had seemed like it was a hundred metres long. In the early evenings, when she carried the yoghurt bowl in two hands across the crowded street, she kept hold of her scarf with her teeth. She was always anxious. She was a seven-year-old girl convinced that the anxiety would never leave her.

Back then, the wall in front her was in the underground

three-by-four metre room she inhabited with her mother. She saw imprints on them all through childhood. She faced the same wall every time she slept, to avoid disturbing her mother as she wove carpets. Her mother's shadow, a figure bent over the carpet, was always on the wall. She wove all day long. She wove for the neighbour's wife, for the carpet businessman. It seemed as if all the world's yarn was gathered in Ranna's mother's home; she never paused her weaving until Alzheimer's finally stilled her hands.

In her sadness and loneliness, Ranna had made imprints of her life on that wall for seventeen years. She would find their old house in Sangcharak in the middle of the stains. It looked warm, with thick white curtains. Inside, she saw her father. He was just like her neighbour in Mashhad, who bought his daughter dresses.

One day, Ranna and the daughter had gone to buy bread together. "Let's take fruit leather from Haji's store," Ranna had said. "Haji won't be able to see us – he's inside the shop."

"My mother said that it is a sin," her neighbour said. "God does not like thieves. God is great. He can always see us. He is powerful. He can do anything He wants."

Ranna said, "Then he is just like my father. He is also powerful – he is doing his jihad. He is doing whatever he wishes. I want to become like him."

The largest stain was always her father. He was tall; his hands were big; he was larger than anything else. He was powerful. Like God, he was not afraid of anyone. He could do whatever he wanted.

Later on, when she was a teenager, the largest stain had begun to divide into smaller ones. Ranna understood it then: her mother was much bigger. She was much stronger. In her silence, she too was like God, who saw things and said nothing. In silence, she too turned bags of yarn into carpets. Maybe God was like her mother. She never raised her voice – not even in fights, not even when Ranna stole fruit leather from Haji's shop.

Today too, as Ranna lay between the bloodied walls and thought of her mother, God was silent. When the explosion had happened and everyone was thrown together into the sky, once again, God did not say a thing.

She wanted to cry. From morning until now, she had felt the need to, but she could not. Only a few drops of tears would flow before immediately drying inside her eyelids. The rest of the drops seemed to be stuck, as if her eyes didn't have the power to let them out.

The voices stopped reaching her ears as her head became slowly empty. The only sounds she could hear were the siren of the ambulance and the noise of the washing of the street.

She had taken everything with her that day. Maybe it was all buried, maybe it was still up in the sky, or maybe the water had taken it down to the Kabul River, flowing towards the Mahmood Khan Bridge, then reaching Macroyan, and finally wishing itself on to Pakistan.

Half of her body was not there. But her purse, half-burnt, sat in the water. Her tazkera was floating on the surface, only one of its corners still intact. A business card had also slipped out of the purse. On it, a few letters, muh . . . di . . ., from "muhandis", were visible, not yet washed away. It was all there, all still floating on the surface.

THE BLACK CROW OF WINTER

Marie Bamyani

Translated from the Dari by Dr Zubair Popalzai

Contrary to the forecast, the weather is not -18°C. It is stuck between -1°C and -5°C. Some people are happy. Everyone keeps saying that, last year, winter was much colder and brought greater misery than this year. People even broke the pipes running through their walls, just to keep the water running.

For her, the temperatures make no difference. Truth be told, she does not know the difference between the numbers. In any case, she must cover herself with the second-hand clothes she was given by the lady next door, to stop the rough, oppressive hand of winter from reaching her aching bones and making her cry out in her sleep.

As usual, she looks at her phone, its screen faded. The clock shows the good hour, four o'clock: time to go home. She frowns, but the lines aren't easy to make out on her sunburnt face. She looks around her and wipes her hands on her dusty grey skirt. She reaches for her collar and takes out a wrinkled piece of cloth that smells like the old sweat of a worker. She puts her hand in her pocket and digs for something at the bottom of it. A few seconds later, she takes out a green fabric triangle, hemmed in white thread. Wrapped within it is a small red book with calligraphy in its margins. She kisses the book and sets it aside. Then she pulls out a yellow five-afghani note.

As she stares at the note, her frown lines become deeper and easier to see. She is brought back to herself by the voice of a man calling her name. "Aunt Zarghoona, why this sad face? What has happened? Why haven't you left for home yet?"

She hurriedly pulls her shawl around her chest and says, "Mudeer sahib, I am just leaving. It is now four o'clock." She tries to iron the frown off her forehead so that the manager does not ask her any more questions.

The manager, a young man in fine clothes, glances around the storeroom, closes the door, and returns to his warm office without waiting for her to finish her answer. She feels opposing currents cross in her mind. She calls, "Mudeer sahib, Mudeer sahib," but the spark is too late.

She picks out crushed cartons and plastic bottles from the bins; she puts them in a sack and leaves it in a corner. She ties on her sun-worn headscarf, its floral patterns barely visible now, and, with all the energy left in her, reaches for the sack.

She hangs back in the storage area for a moment so she may leave through the gate unseen.

She has not yet passed through the gate before she is overcome by the thought of having to walk the crowded and garbage-laden road from Cinema-e-Pamir to Qala-e-Zaman Khan, listening to the noise of pedlars and the cursing of passers-by. It multiplies the weight she is carrying. She curses herself for not thinking a little sooner to borrow ten afghanis from the mudeer. But in her heart, she is happy that he did not hear her and left before she could talk to him. She also prays that she will be lucky and the cleaner of a van will give her a free ride. Then she remembers how many times she has been cursed at or even thrown out of a van for not having the money to pay the fare. All these thoughts make her lose hope again.

Because of the cold, the city feels like a steel plant. Workers warm their rough hands over barrels of fire placed on the footpath of the river, Darya-ye Kabul, as though they are shielding rubies from which high flames and smoke rise. The smoke is so intense it is difficult to see the outline of the Cinema-e Pamir building. Vendors and shopkeepers are so busy haggling with buyers, ignoring the cold, that even the passer-by forgets its icy burn for a moment.

She counts the days and finds there are only ten more to the end of the month. But even when each month ends, her problems are not answered. She knows she cannot afford to buy food every day for her family of six, let alone her daily fare to get to work, which has now increased to ten afghanis. Her four young daughters all go to school and her ten-year-old son sits with his blind father at the gate every evening to greet her. Liaqat is always restless for his mother's arrival. He hopes that maybe one day she will bring home a lollipop for him, like the ones he watches the neighbour's child lick each day. A few times, the boy has shared his lollipop with Liaqat, out of pure kindness.

The hands of the clock are running faster than she is walking. It feels as if time itself is fed up with her – her thoughts, her complaints and the stench of her sweat. It is fed up with her sitting at the roadside to take a break, and even with the occasional insults hurled at her by bus conductors.

The clock shows 5.45 p.m. She has just arrived in Dehburi. She puts her sack on the floor and leans against a lamp post at the edge of the street. She breathes calmly for a few minutes. She envies the potted flowers and grass planted in the middle of the road, lying quiet amid all the noise. She shifts her eyes and stares at the tyres that pass in front of her like the wind. She remembers the smell of hot bread coming from her neighbour's oven in the morning and the grumpy voice of the baker's husband, cursing his wife. From time to time, she tries flagging down a passing car, hoping that the kindest driver will give her a lift and help her carry her load. Her exhaustion has stolen her serenity. She cannot stand on her legs. They are refusing to walk her home. Deep in her heart, she wishes for an explosion to tear her body into pieces and free her from this wretched life forever. Then she remembers her children and her husband, curses herself, and utters, "God, you are great."

The sun has set into the furthest corners, leaving the earth alone in the dark grey smoke dancing from the chimneys. One can hardly see or put a face to a voice one metre away. But her gaze is fixed on the passing vehicles as she tries to flag them down. She shouts, "Please stop, for the sake of good deeds, and take me with you!"

She knows how unlikely it is. The high-end cars that flash from five metres away to pick up cute girls will not stop for her. Once, when she did get a lift, she was so enchanted by the soft, chocolate-coloured seats of the car that she could not even make out what the driver was saying. She sat straight, trying not to lean back and soil the soft seat with her dirty, stinking clothes. The gentle perfume, the warm air and the sound of music had taken her into a dream, a fleeting dream indeed – cut short when the driver threw her out of the car, making an excuse about an emergency.

She smiles now at the thought of that beautiful dream. Then she begins again, calling out to the drivers who are crowding the streets of the city:

"Please stop, take me with you, for the sake of good deeds!"

"Stop please, take me with you, for good deeds."

This time her voice reaches a conductor. He is eighteen or nineteen, with a shawl wrapped like a square around his head, to protect against dust and the noise of passengers. He spits thick saliva onto the road and shouts to the driver in a rough voice:

"Khalifa, stop for the rider. Run, Khala, hurry up."

Like a six- or seven-year-old girl, she becomes excited. She jumps up happily and grabs her sack, which now feels so much lighter. She runs towards the vehicle. As a sign of gratitude, she smiles at the conductor, suddenly revealing her fine front teeth.

The seats inside the van are all taken by passengers with desperate looks, dust-covered clothes and untidy hair. She is not bothered by their exhausted faces or the lack of available seats. She puts her sack down and sits on it.

She holds out the note in her hand to the conductor. "Please charge me five afghanis. I don't have ten."

The conductor smiles at her. "Don't you worry, Khala Jan. Keep it for yourself."

She pulls her hand back happily and holds more tightly on to the note, so that she will not lose it. She leans her head against the window and closes her eyes. She looks forward to her destination, thinking that today she will buy a coloured sugar-water lollipop for her son.

SILVER RING

Freshta Ghani

Translated from the Pashto by Shekiba Habib

We were playing the same old game of hopscotch – me, my friend Zarghoona and her sister Spozhmai. The rules are simple: we kick a small pebble from one of the seven heptagons we have drawn on the ground to another heptagon. If a foot or the pebble touches one of the lines, then that player is out and it is the next person's turn.

Now, Zarghoona – who'd been hopping from one heptagon to another – was out and they were both telling me it was my turn.

I looked at my muddy feet and felt embarrassed. I remained where I was, with one foot behind the other. Zarghoona and Spozhmai lived across the street from me. Their feet were healthy and soft, and they were wearing new sandals. My sandals were plastic and hand-stitched by my mother. But I felt even worse about my feet, which were dry and dirty. They didn't look good at all.

I turned and ran across the courtyard, past the mud walls of the dusty room we used as a makeshift kitchen, and into the bathroom at the far end of the yard. One half of the floor was paved with concrete while the other half was muddy.

I realised that the old soap was finished and there was no money for new soap. I looked down at my feet, covered with mud and cracked because of the cold. I began to scrub them hard with the little loofah but couldn't get them clean.

I didn't want to go out anymore.

When I came out of the bathroom, my mother was in the courtyard, wearing her burqa.

"Where are you going?" I said.

She glared at me.

"Moor Jani, where are you going?"

"Shopping! Why so many questions?"

"I wanted to tell you that we have run out of soap. Will you buy some?"

"On top of taking care of your hungry stomach, now I have to think of soap too," she said.

I lowered my head and said nothing. She was turning the silver ring on her finger. It had a bluish stone set in a double shank. I didn't like it very much. My father had brought it back for her when he'd returned home after a long spell in the army. I'd seen her talking to that ring when he was away. She would even cry and sing to it.

Once, I heard my mother tell my aunt, "This ring is very precious to me. Even when I die I won't have it taken off my finger. I will wear it on judgement day. It is my first marriage gift."

My mother left without another word while I leaned against the doorway watching her go. In my heart, I wished I were Zarghoona's sister, so I could have new sandals, and soap to wash my hands and feet.

I looked at the clock. It seemed as though the hands hadn't moved since my mother left. My two little sisters and brother were crying for food. I was very hungry too. We hadn't eaten anything since morning. My hands and legs were shaking and the room seemed to be spinning. My older sister, Samina, sat next to the window with her hand under her chin. I knew she was even more worried than me. I lay down on the mattress on the floor and closed my eyes but my hunger kept me awake.

When I looked at the clock again it was quarter past three in the afternoon. Moor had left home before ten that morning. I began wondering where she'd gone.

I must have drifted off to sleep because I had a dream in which I was sitting in a room full of women baking bread. I reached out and took a piece but it slipped from my hand and dropped into a deep black hole. I threw myself after it, but it had disappeared.

A sharp knock on the door woke me. I jumped to my feet and answered it. It was Zarghoona holding a big doll in her hand. "Come, Dunya, let's play. Aba just brought me this."

Zarghoona's doll had bright yellow hair and a round face. My mind took me back to the time when my father used to bring us gifts, and the day I realised he would never do so again. I remembered the afternoon when the courtyard door was suddenly pushed open by my uncle Rahim, dressed in black, his top and trousers muddy. He was accompanied by four men in military uniform. He rushed into the house and called out to my mother. She didn't answer. I don't think she heard him.

Uncle Rahim opened both sides of the front door and I saw that four military men were carrying a long wooden box. My uncle called again, and Moor came out.

"Sister-in-law," Uncle Rahim said, "may God give you patience. Sharif is martyred!"

When my mother saw the box with my father's body in it, she crumpled in a heap on the floor. I ran towards the box, called out to my father and tried to shake him awake. Then I began screaming. The neighbours came and dragged me away.

"Come on, Dunya, let's play." Zarghoona was poking my shoulder.

"No," I said, wiping my eyes. "Not today. Maybe tomorrow."

"Why not? Come on, please! I will ask your mother for permission."

I shook my head and forced a smile. "I have a bit of a temperature. I need to lie down. I'll play with you tomorrow."

I stayed beside the door when Zarghoona left. The street was full of the shouts of kids playing. A man's voice rose up above the noise: "Cheese, fresh cheese". Then came the music from the ice cream cart. I began desperately wishing for an ice cream. I imagined Zarghoona and Spozhmai running off to buy some. I peered through the little hole in the courtyard door but could see nothing. I turned and went back inside the house.

The time for evening prayer came and went. The sun slowly dragged its rays across the houses. Sabrina, my second sister, and my little brother, Zyarat Gul, had fallen asleep.

I stretched out on the floor and began counting the rafters. After my father died, we moved to this old mud house. There were two rooms, one of which was very dusty, the ceiling ruined. The other room was a bit better, so we lived there. But whenever it got mouldy and damp from the rains, little bugs would drop on us from the ceiling.

I counted fifteen rafters. I counted them again, then counted them from the other side. I did this over and over to pass the time.

There was another knock on the courtyard door, but I didn't have the energy to answer it. Sabrina jumped to her feet and ran so fast to get to it that she fell over in the yard. She got back up, her knee bleeding, and pulled open the door. Sabrina was so delicate, and would cry at the smallest thing. But today hunger had toughened her.

A kilo of rice – that was all we were waiting for Moor to bring us, so we could cook and eat. There was not even a potato left. The previous day we had boiled the last four. Our flour container had been empty for a long time. It was the year of the mouse, the season of meagreness.

Before, it used to be a little easier for my mother. She washed people's clothes, was paid a small amount of money, and we survived. But for a whole week she could barely move because of the pain in her lower back which meant she couldn't work. We started praying to God.

When Sabrina opened the courtyard door we all sat up, expecting Moor. She came back to the room and told Samina that it was the landlord asking for the monthly rent. Samina asked me to go and tell him that we would pay the following day.

I went out and said to him, "My mother is not at home, she will pay you when she is here."

"This is the fifth month that you haven't paid me," he shouted. His mouth was full of spit and green tobacco, which stained his long beard. "I will come next week, and if you don't pay me, I will throw all your things into the street."

A nearby shopkeeper came out of his shop. The neighbours also came out. They were all staring at me. Worse still, the street boys began laughing. "Uncle Jabbar, they are tricking you. They will not pay you any rent."

The landlord shouted even more loudly. "I swear, when I come back next time, I will throw you out if you do not pay."

I fixed my eyes on my feet. I felt the heat rising to my face. I decided there and then that when I grew up I would get a job and earn good money and throw the rent money in his face. I shut the door and turned back.

I was halfway across the yard when I heard another knock at the door. The door opened and this time a tall, forty-year-old woman stood there. She looked exhausted. So much dust covered her sandals that they had lost all colour. She had a plastic bag in her hand with pale white rice clearly visible through it. My sweet mother! The woman whose tears would never dry!

Samina hurried out to meet her, took the bag and told us she was going to cook.

I followed Moor into the room. I watched the movements of her hands as she removed her blue burqa. Zyarat Gul came in and she reached down and lifted him to her shoulder, stroking his short hair. I saw Sabrina and Samina through the kitchen door, busy preparing the rice. I left the room, sat on the floor and watched.

This final hour seemed to have no end while I waited. It was late evening when the food was ready.

We ate our fill, then the younger ones fell quietly asleep.

I was lying in bed, still awake, when I heard Samina say softly, "Moor Jani, did you borrow this rice?" Samina's voice was anxious.

"No. They said they would not lend to me until I paid off what I already owed them. They won't give me anything."

"Then how did you get the rice?"

Moor said nothing for a while, then her voice dropped to a whisper. "Don't tell anyone, Samina: I sold my silver ring."

"But that was—"

"Be quiet, don't let anyone know."

"But who would buy it, Moor Jani? The stone wasn't real."

"That's why they paid only sixty afghanis. I bought two kilos of rice with the money."

Samina began sobbing quietly and I couldn't hold my tears back either.

Moor reached across and tapped me sharply on the back. "Go to sleep, Dunya! You'll wake up the little ones."

SANDALS

Maliha Naji

*Translated from the Pashto by Shekiba Habib
and Zarghuna Kargar*

Wisps of hair poked through a hole in her long red scarf. She came up close to the man and passed him the mug she held in her blackened fingers. She said, "Gul Ahmad! My back is aching. Please bring back a tub of Vicks – the one that has a picture of a spine on it. The pain is excruciating, I can't bend down to put bread in the tanoor. It's like my back is breaking."

Gul Ahmad knelt and raised the mug to his mouth, his black moustache touching its edges. "Oof, this is so bitter, like poison. Go and get me some gur if there's any left."

Zarmina's dry heels scraped the drugget as she walked. She said crossly, "I wish these feet would get lost. I can't even walk – my heart shrieks. May these cracked heels go to hell."

Gul Ahmad burst out laughing. "Is there any part of your body that doesn't have something wrong with it?"

Zarmina curled her lip and turned her face away. She pulled a bunch of keys from her chest and unlocked the box. She slipped her fingers into a bag inside it, then held her hand out to her husband. "Is it enough?"

Gul Ahmad looked at her. "Yes, just enough to help me swallow this tea."

"We are almost out of gur. I put some in the halwa when your elder brother was here and we've run out. If any guest comes, we will be embarrassed. Your brothers' wives won't lend me anything. To hell with poverty."

"Oh woman, have some patience! God is giving us enough to eat morning and night. So far, we haven't had to ask anyone for help. I hope God will have mercy on us and these days will also pass. Don't think about it now. I can just afford to buy shoes for your sons."

"Merra! Lashta's sandals are also torn. The weather is cold. She runs around with the other children all day long, and her toes turn red. Buy her a pair of plastic shoes too – but don't get a big size, they will make too much noise when she walks." She showed him the span of her hand. "One champa is enough for her."

Her husband looked doubtful. "I will check my pockets. If I get this work, then the money should be good this time. Give me another half cup of tea. I mustn't be late."

Gul Ahmad worked for a company in Kabul, selling paper

serviettes and mineral water to shops. Sometimes the work was good but at other times he did not earn much. He called to his sons, on his way out. "Ghorzang, Naseer! Come here, boys."

Ghorzang and Naseer ran to him with dusty feet. They had been playing with their cousins in the yard.

"Yes, Aba!"

"Come here so I can measure your feet."

"Aba, I will bring the thread. Last time, you measured with your hands and the shoes were too tight."

Gul Ahmad fixed his black turban on his head and called Zarmina. She rushed over, her skirt flaring, to hand him the roll of black thread.

Gul Ahmad measured both boys' feet and put the threads in his pocket. The edges of his waistcoat shone and his hair lit up with the sunlight when he took his turban off for a moment. He rubbed his head, fixed his hat back on and wrapped the turban around it, tucking in the edges. He walked down the passage, calling, "Zarmina! I am going. I'll be back on Thursday. The weather is getting cold, I can't survive in the room there."

Zarmina was ready, holding the bucket of water to throw after him. "Alright, have a safe journey!"

Gul Ahmad walked through the gate. The water hit the ground behind him. He strode through the village and in a few seconds he had disappeared. Zarmina stood in the doorway looking in the direction he had gone, sadness in her face. A cloud drifted across the sun.

*

Days and nights passed. Zarmina groaned and held her lower back as she bent down to the oven.

"This damned pain! I wish I had an older daughter who could do the household chores for me. Then, like Zarmin Gul, I would be fine."

She wrapped two thin breads in a cloth, put some butter on a small plate and walked towards the children. Her two sons and Lashta were sitting at the far end of the room, amid the clicking of small bright marbles. Zarmina called, "Come here, leave the marbles and eat this bread and butter. You'll be playing till lunchtime – you won't be able to run around if you don't eat."

Ghorzang came forward and opened the cloth that contained the bread. Naseer sat cross-legged. Chubby Lashta also sat down, pushed her messy curls away from her forehead, rubbed her eyes and yawned. Zarmina watched her. "Quick, quick, you are six years old, what's wrong with you? Get up and wash your face!"

They all sat around the cloth, each one taking small scoops from the dollop of butter. Zarmina was deep in her own thoughts. Then she said, "Ghorzang! What day is today? I have lost track of the days. Your father is coming home on Thursday."

"Today is Thursday, Adey, but isn't Aba usually away a week longer? It's early yet."

"Oh, it's Thursday already! It feels like he went yesterday. I wish I had counted the days. This is what happens when you are not educated – I should have known how to mark the day. I haven't prepared anything. Tomorrow is Friday and there is a prayer meal at Qazi Farid's house."

There was a knock at the door. Ghorzang put some bread in his mouth as Zarmina said, "Hurry up, son! It could be your father."

"Adey! It's only half past eight. It could be Batoor. We have a cricket match with the boys from the lower village."

As he opened the door, the chain clanged against the wooden frame. The boy stuck his head out. "Hey, who knocked on our door?"

It was a big village. Grey smoke rose from some of the houses. In the distance, old trees stood tall on the slopes that surrounded the village. The sun shone against a bright blue sky and a light breeze passed in the air. Four boys stood, hot and sweating, rubbing their cracked hands. One of them shouted, "Ghorzang, it was Samsor, he went to let the others know too. Let's go, or we'll be late again."

"Wait, let me put my socks on, I will be right there."

Ghorzang quickly climbed the four steps back to the house and rushed across the landing. There was a noise of cups falling. "Careful, son," Zarmina said, angrily. "You broke the cups."

Ghorzang and Naseer ran out again. The door closed behind them.

The clock showed ten o'clock. Zarmina sat out in the yard, her hair seeming blacker in the sun. She held the corner of her grey scarf between her teeth as she brushed Lashta's golden hair. She kissed her daughter on her head and spoke kindly to her. "I don't know who you've taken after, you golden-haired girl. Neither my hair nor Aba's is this colour."

"Adey, my aunt's hair and Gul uncle's is golden."

"Mother's love, you are from the same clan. Now be careful not to get your hands and feet dirty; tomorrow we'll be going to the prayer meal."

Lashta touched her hair, her chubby fingers bright in the sunshine.

"Adey, will we have Pepsi?"

"No, zama grani, it's cold now, there won't be Pepsi."

"What about meat?"

"Yes, my child, there will be meat in the rice."

"Adey, I will go outside but I won't touch anything dirty."

Lashta stood up and went down the stairs, hopping all the way. Zarmina stretched out her legs, calling: "Slowly, slowly, leave the gate open for your father."

Zarmina continued to sit there, her legs stretched out on the rug. She leaned against the wall and breathed in deeply as the sun warmed her heels. She watched the scattered clouds in the blue sky, enjoying the sunshine and the freshness of the air, but the light was soon too bright for her eyes, so she looked down and disappeared into her thoughts.

She only looked up again when the gate opened and Gul Ahmad entered with a big sack. "Zama khaza, come and take these cauliflowers and oranges."

Zarmina ran towards him. "Are you well? Welcome home."

"Yes, come and take these, the rest you can deal with later."

Zarmina took the produce into the house. She threw a bag of tomatoes into the blackened cooking pan. Gul Ahmad lay on the mattress, removed his black turban and put it by the window. "Bring me some tea. The weather is getting so cold, the wind blows up one's nose."

"Here, take the tea. We have fresh milk too, shall I bring some?"

"No, no, it's close to lunchtime, it won't taste nice. Take a look at these shoes. Call the children."

"Ghorzang and Naseer are not here, they are by the river. The boys from the lower village have invited them for a match. Lashta is behind the house. Ogay's uncle and family have come for Qazi Farid's prayer meal."

Zarmina's eyes glowed with happiness as she looked through the things Gul Ahmad had brought. She smiled and exclaimed, "My God, you brought Lashta Kabuli trainers!"

"Yes, they were relatively cheap and warm too. I said, why not, I have only one daughter."

Through the big window, Gul Ahmad looked out at the mountain. There was silence. No birds sang in the trees, the sun hid behind grey clouds. In the yard, golden leaves drifted down to the ground from the big tree.

He took a big sip of tea. Before he had set his cup down he heard the bang. The glass of the window shattered. The air was filled with the sound of birds screeching as they took off, the ground painted in the autumn colours of fallen leaves.

"God help us, that was close."

Gul Ahmad was out first, Zarmina behind him, both running on bare feet. There was smoke everywhere. Gul Ahmad coughed as the smell of gunpowder scorched his nose.

All the men and women were standing in the middle of the village. Gul Ahmad rubbed his eyes as he ran.

His heart beat strangely as he moved forwards into the crowd. Zarmina stood pale, heart clenched, unable to breathe. Everything had gone quiet; no birds perched on the bare branches. The air over the village was so full of smoke that it hid the mountain. Clouds covered half the sky.

Then the sun slowly spread its rays. Gul Ahmad took two more steps, very carefully. His feet touched something. He stopped and knelt by the blood-soaked body. Lashta was taking her last breath.

Gul Ahmad and Zarmina stood by the lifeless body of their only daughter.

THE WORMS

Fatima Saadat

The ticking of the wall clock might have hypnotised her mother into a deep sleep, but it was keeping Zohra awake as usual. Their little room was slowly getting darker as the solar lamp started to die. Her mother stirred, and shouted to her to turn it off and save some power for tomorrow. She got up to switch it off, then scurried back to her side of the room. She turned away from the window, quickly pulling a thin flowery blanket up over her face to shut out the darkness.

It was two-thirty in the morning when her eyes finally closed, but at the same time something inside her awoke. She felt a coldness in her feet, and found that something wet and soft was rubbing against her toes. When she tried to look, all she could see was darkness. She tried to move her legs, but her body was frozen. And then she felt herself being pulled suddenly and forcefully from within, a twisting force squeezing her chest and making her struggle to breathe. Zohra tried to shout out and move her limbs, but her body would not obey her. Each time she would fall back into the blackness, as if she were being pulled down into the depths of a well, beyond where her eyes could see. She was afraid that if she gave in to it, she would never return to the surface, and she recalled her mother's advice to recite the name of God when in need. She whispered, *Allah, Allah, Allah* . . . The words appeared before her, then vanished as quickly as they had appeared.

She sat bolt upright and threw the blanket away. She was covered in sweat. She turned on the flashlight of her phone and pointed it towards her feet. A long, dark brown worm was writhing in pain, half of its body ground into the rug beneath her.

When Zohra next awoke, it was to the peaceful, fresh scent of the morning breeze and the familiar sound of her mother sweeping their dusty yard. Her mother, Hakima, wore a long green cotton dress with tiny flowers on it, and white trousers with detailed khamak that she had embroidered herself down the sides. Although she was only in her thirties, hardship and loneliness had given her tired skin and greying hair. She still kept her hair long, and it covered her back.

Hakima walked over to the small glass bottles of home-made torshi, cucumber pickles and chatni sauce that were lined up in a shaded corner of the tiny yard, ready to be picked up by the seller man.

"I heard you moaning last night," Hakima said to Zohra in a still voice. "You had Bakhtak attacking you again? I told you that you must wash your hands and mouth after you eat meat at night." Zohra had picked up a piece of broken mirror and was inspecting her face, prodding the acne on her chin. She occasionally glanced at her mother, but said nothing. Hakima started collecting the small pieces of cloth that were drying on branches, and tried again to get a response from her daughter. "You never talk about your dreams. You should have taken the mullah's amulet – taken his message, folded the paper small and strung it around your neck. Or we could soak it in water for you to drink. Yes, that would help."

Zohra looked away from the mirror and through the bedroom window, staring at the purple and white vases on the windowsill inside. She turned to look squarely at her mother and said: "Nanai, when I was a child, we used to live in a house with a big garden, right? I vaguely remember it. I used to bring you dead, dried-up worms, didn't I?"

"What? No, I don't remember such a thing. I do remember the day I pulled a cockroach out of your mouth, though!" Her mother laughed, not looking at her, and continued to gather up the washing. She handed a few pieces of cloth to Zohra. "Here, dried and clean. Hide them somewhere until you get your next cycle."

"Nanai! Why are you like this? Why do you always avoid any conversation about the garden house?"

"What on earth are you talking about? What conversations? I don't know what's got into you recently."

"Just any conversation – proper ones, real ones!" Zohra went back into the house, slamming the door behind her.

Hakima stared at her wrinkled and dirty hands and saw that they were shaking.

It was around noon when the bell rang, marking the last of the morning lessons. The male students – especially the juniors – ran and jostled their way across the dusty schoolyard to their next class. Zohra was walking towards her lesson, which was in a room on the second floor, just by the outdoor stairs. She stopped in front of the classroom door with its sign that read "Seventh grade B, girls", and looked at the morning glory with its purple flowers, twisting around the white iron bars of the stairs. One tendril had grown long and floated out into the air. For a second, she saw the stems turn to claws that grabbed at her, she heard the screams of a woman, and she felt footsteps thumping in her chest. She stepped backwards and was knocked down by one of the younger boys. Zohra watched him run away quickly as she got up and dusted off her black uniform.

Her books and papers had been scattered, the wind blowing them across the schoolyard. Everyone was peering down at the pages with shocked expressions on their faces.

"Hey, hey. What happened here? Did someone push you again, Zohra? Amina, come here. Help her."

Ustad Hafiz, the stick-thin principle, picked up one of the pages, gazed at it, let go of the small boy's ear that he was pulling, and shook his head in disappointment. He stared at the unfamiliar shapes and figures on the paper: giant black worms between wild branches of trees.

All the students started whispering.

"Nobody pushed me, Ustad. I slipped," Zohra said quietly.

"I am not touching her stuff, Ustad," Amina said in her reedy voice. She became more animated. "In fact, I don't want to be in the same class as her. My mother says she has jinn inside her." Amina lived next door to Zohra. Sometimes, Zohra would hear Zahir, Amina's father, blow his nose so hard and loud that, as she had once told her mother, she worried he would blow his brain out through his nose.

"Everybody go to your classes; the show is over." Ustad Hafiz collected the few remaining papers and handed them to Zohra. He said to her quietly, "I think you should stop drawing. All you do – all day – is draw. You nearly failed calculus. You are disappointing me, Zohra. Drawing won't help kids like you. Afghanistan needs female presidents, female politicians, female engineers and female economists. Go focus on physics, or geometry or chemistry." Zohra raised her eyebrows just enough that he wouldn't notice as he embarked on another speech on the future of Afghanistan. His chapped lips moved up and down; white froth built up at the corners of his mouth as he talked. "Do you hear me, Zohra? Now go to your class."

She held her drawings tightly in her arms as she hurried to her next lesson.

Zohra was staring at the blackboard as the class representative announced that their teacher was absent again, and the students started cheering. Azima, who was sitting next to Zohra, took a piece of damp cloth from her bag and started cleaning the dust from her shoes. She offered another piece to Zohra to clean her trousers.

"Zohra, do you want to come with me to Ms Sharifi's office? She gives good advice." The other girl's voice was friendly.

"You mean the Love Confessions office?" asked a voice from the front row, as Humaira turned her head to reveal a mocking smile before gazing again at her reflection in her pocket mirror.

"Ha. Funny," Azima said. "Not everyone is like you, with your boy problems. Some people have other things to worry about – bigger things."

"I'm fine. I don't have time for it," Zohra interjected. "I need to focus on calculus before midterm exams start." Zohra looked down and pretended to read.

"Focusing on your studies? How? By not sleeping at night? By having constant headaches? Girl, you need to speak to someone. Open up a bit." She leaned a little closer to Zohra. "Did your mother say anything about your father—"

"Azima! Enough. Why do you have to tell everyone?"

"Have I ever told anyone anything?" Azima said, her tone shifting. She paused for a moment. "OK, I will leave you be if I'm such a bother. See you around."

Azima got up and pulled the wet cloth out of Zohra's hand. Zohra kept staring at the blurry lines of the book she was holding, squeezing its pages hard.

The sound of the azan broke through the dark blue and orange atmosphere of the evening, and the first star of the night could be seen in the distance. The smell of onion and tomatoes filled the alley, where you could guess what each neighbour was having to eat. Hakima put the lid on the pot and went into the yard for wuzu and prayers, leaving Zohra to pace the room.

Zohra had stopped counting her sleepless nights long ago. She hated that something so ordinary had become so difficult. These nightmares were never going to let her be normal, she thought to herself. She walked quickly up to the cupboard where she kept her papers and pencils, took out all of her materials, and threw them into a black plastic bag. The principal's words kept echoing in her head: *We do not need female artists. Focus on your studies.*

Hakima wiped away her tears as she stared at Zohra through the window, whispering prayers with her hand raised in front of her, looking up occasionally at the sky. When Zohra caught her mother's gaze, Hakima quickly looked the other way.

Zohra crushed the white papers in her fists. She wanted to shout, but nothing came out, and her tears refused to fall. Instead, there was just a dark cloud around her head.

"Bachim, the food is ready. Let's eat dinner," her mother shouted.

Zohra ignored her and lay down, covering her face with her blanket.

Zohra starts to walk slowly towards the big trees at the end of their garden. They smell different at night. They look different in darkness. She is barefoot, and her feet are numb with the cold, covered in mud. She can feel the worms and damp leaves moving beneath her when she drops to her hands and knees and crawls on the floor. As she makes her way towards the apricot trees, the darkness deepens and the air becomes thicker. The sound of her parents arguing comes as always from the house. She starts to cry, and the sound twists between the branches, in and out of their shadows. She can feel her body suddenly growing in size, her surroundings getting smaller and tighter. She lies on the floor gasping for air, gazing at the monstrous claws of the trees merging into one giant hand rushing towards her. She wants to give up this time. She closes her eyes and lets herself sink into the darkness. Then something pulls her up, and she finds herself in the arms of her mother, swaddled in a thin scarf. She pulls back the material from her face and looks back over her mother's shoulder to see the hands of a man chasing her. A motorbike roars, and the figure, the trees and the darkness grow more distant.

"Wake up, Zohra. Wake up. Open your eyes, my daughter." Hakima had tears in her eyes as she hugged her and kissed her head. She sat beside her and held Zohra's hands in hers. "I'm sorry. I'm sorry for leaving you alone with him in that house. It was just once. Your father had beaten me and forced me out. He wouldn't let me come back." She stroked Zohra's forehead, looking deep into her eyes. "Then I heard he wanted to sell you."

Zohra looked at her mother.

"I came back, just for you," Hakima continued. "And I promised that I would never leave you alone again."

Zohra remembered how her mother would hold her tight as they lay by the apricot trees and looked up at the branches as the wind shook them. She remembered her mother's beautiful long thick black hair, which would occasionally escape her orange zari dozi scarf. She remembered her smile, the lullabies she used to sing to her, and the soft hands that would caress her.

"Please know that I had no other choice. I had to escape him, and the village, before they killed me for running away. I did it for us."

She remembered her father beating her mother as she screamed for help. She remembered hiding in the bathroom and pressing her little hands so hard to her ears that they hurt.

Zohra looked again at her mother and saw the same beautiful woman, one with a crooked smile and tears in her eyes. "I know." She held her mother's bony hands and kissed them.

Zohra ran her fingers along the walls of the school as she walked. She felt them become warm and numb after a few steps. She looked at her hands, opened her arms and embraced the wall, looking up to the sky. It was almost sunset, and the last rays of the sun were fading on the newly painted cement wall. She pressed herself against it, closed her eyes, and smiled as she smelled the fresh paint.

Azima came over to her as she collected the dirty brushes.

"Hey, are you licking the wall again? Is it dry?" Azima said, pressing on Zohra's right shoulder.

"Not dry enough that the smell of paint has gone. Want to try?"

They both laughed and looked at the mural they had just painted. It was a girl in a light blue uniform, holding books and pencils in one arm, her other arm raised upwards, touching a rainbow over her head.

Hakima woke in the middle of the night to the sound of footsteps. She saw a dark shape moving in the corner of her eyes. The shadow moved quickly towards the yard. Her heartbeat quickened. What would she do if it were thieves? There was no man in the house. She grabbed the small torch from under her pillow and crawled slowly to the window. The shadow was moving back and forth. She pointed the light at it and saw a familiar figure.

"For god's sake! What are you doing out here in the middle of the night? I thought it was thieves or balla."

Zohra turned to her mother, holding the purple vase in her hands. She said calmly, "I think it is better for it to be out here, rather than inside on the windowsill. Its soil contains worms. It should be outside, in the garden."

Hakima sighed as she made her way back to her bed. She lay down on her side, looking out of the window, squinting to see her daughter better. Zohra was still holding the vase, her gazed fixed on it, as little worms crawled on the ground.

KHURSHID KHANUM, RISE AND SHINE

Batool Haidari

*Translated from the Dari by Parwana Fayyaz
and Dr Zubair Popalzai*

He called but nobody answered. He tried the number again and again throughout the day, but all he could hear was the sound of the phone ringing. He couldn't remember the last time she had stayed out for so long. He speculated. Maybe Khurshid is ill. Maybe something else has caused her to stop answering the phone.

Someone finally picked up around nine that evening. He could not breathe when he heard her say, "Hello?"

When he was a student in Kabul and was engaged to Alia, he would call her and wait silently for her to initiate the conversation. He had wanted to hear her heartbeat. Every time it was the same: he never spoke first. Alia had come to expect this, so instead of saying "Hello," she would giggle, then ask, "Suleiman, is that you?"

The woman on the phone did not giggle. Sounding frustrated, she asked if he had stomach cramps that were stopping him from talking. Tears dried in his eyes. He could not remember Alia ever answering so harshly.

He remembered that for a time they had had a regular ghost caller. The person would call, then keep silent. Suleiman had sworn at them on a few occasions, but it had proven futile. Alia was of the opinion that there was no justification for profanity even if the caller called a hundred times and said nothing.

This time she had not cursed. She had said, "Do you have stomach cramps?" When the call disconnected, he redialled the number. His hands were not shaking this time. He was pressing the numbers hard.

The woman on the phone said, "Hello," loudly. He took a deep breath and asked, "Is Alia there?"

He realised that the woman could not have been Alia. She had stretched the word *hello* and said it loudly; Alia never did either.

He sighed in relief when the woman said, "No, you have dialled the wrong number."

But as soon as he put the phone down, he asked himself if this could be true. No – there was no way he had dialled the wrong number. He felt confident about this. He rang again and this time spoke with more confidence to the woman at the other end. He introduced himself as a distant relation of

Alia who had come from one of the provinces to speak to her about something important.

When the woman was reassured that it was not a nuisance call, she explained that they had bought the house from a family three years earlier. He asked the name of the family and the woman replied, "Akbari. Zargham Akbari."

Removing any possible doubt, she said, "Engineer Akbari."

She could not have known that the caller at the other end of the phone was about to faint. She continued talking to "Alia's distant relative", explaining that she did not know exactly where the family lived but knew that they were in Chawk-e Gulha, an upmarket neighbourhood.

Suleiman swallowed hard and asked the woman if she was certain that Engineer Akbari's wife's name was Alia. The woman laughed and confirmed it was. She mentioned Alia's elder daughter, Khurshid.

"A wonderful girl," she said. "I wanted her to be my daughter-in-law, but fate disagreed. She was going to university and my son did not want a wife who went to university."

Suleiman started to sweat profusely when he heard the woman sigh and say, "What has the world come to? The daughters of the martyred are going to university."

He did not understand. He asked, with difficulty, "The martyr's daughter? What martyr?"

The woman was enjoying having someone to speak to. She said, "What kind of family member are you if you are unaware of this, dear brother?"

He tried to think of an explanation, but without waiting for a reply the woman continued, "I don't know much. Her neighbours said that she is a martyr's daughter. That her mother lost her husband and, two years later, married one of her husband's comrades, an engineer. God has now graced her with another child. When we bought the house, she had just given birth. To a beautiful boy called Suleiman."

He could not breathe. He murmured, "Suleiman." Then he hung up.

Floored, he stared motionless at the photograph in his hand. He could not believe that his wife had remarried. That little Khurshid was a university student. That he was thought to have been martyred. That his friend Zargham was now Alia's husband and they had named their son after him. He felt a pain in his throat and pressed his lips together.

The next day, he got out of bed and opened the window. He picked up the water jug and drank from it directly, water spilling on his chest as he gulped. He poured the remainder on his head before going back to bed. He wished he had held his tongue back then – that he had never spoken to Zargham about his wife, never described her to him. He ran his fingers through his greying hair. It had been six years since he was captured. He was relieved he hadn't visited the house yet – all the neighbours would have recognised him. He closed his eyes, a lump in his throat. Then he stood up and stared at the phone. He dialled the number again and the same screeching woman answered.

"Why did you hang up, brother?" she asked. Without waiting for an answer, she continued, "I called Ms Sabri, one of the Akbaris' old neighbours, to tell her that their relative had called. She didn't know exactly where they are living. Just that they live in Chawk-e Gulha, as I told you. But she did say that on Fridays Alia goes to the Martyrs' Cemetery on the hill."

"An old lady used to live with them. Do you know what happened—"

The woman interrupted. "Are you talking about Bibi Jan? She was ill and the neighbours said she had a stroke when she learned of her son's martyrdom. Her heart was broken and she stopped speaking altogether. The poor lady passed away a year later."

When the woman had hung up, Suleiman leaned against the nearest wall and began to sob. It was morning before he opened his eyes again.

On Thursday, he went to the city for a walk. He went to all the places he had visited with Alia and Khurshid. To relive the good old memories, he sat where they had sat before as a family.

In the evening, he went to have his beard shaved. It tickled when the barber ran clippers over the curly hair on his neck. He remembered Alia telling him after their engagement that she did not want him to shave his beard, because a woman's beauty lies in her long hair and a man's beauty and masculinity lie in his beard and moustache. He saw a sparkle in Alia's eyes when he grew a beard for the first time. She would compliment him, telling him that the beard suited him and that he looked like an angel.

He remembered Alia painting. She was working on a painting of angels in those days; they were all men with long hair. He reminded Alia that there are also female angels, but his words fell on deaf ears. When the painting was complete, she wrapped it up and gave it to him as a gift.

Suleiman's beard was now shaven. All that was left was his moustache. He touched it. When the barber asked repeatedly if he should shave the moustache too, Suleiman looked up and asked, "Do you think a moustache suits me?" The barber removed the cape, tapped him on his back and said, "A man without a moustache is not a real man." Suleiman laughed and got up from the chair to look in the mirror. He could not recognise himself.

He left for the cemetery early the next morning. The security office was closed and he had to search the Martyrs' Cemetery himself. Although he had examined every grave, he had not found his name. So now he was waiting for the office to open. A few hours had passed. He lay under a willow tree with his small bag under his head, gazing at the branches hanging down. He had had to search widely even to find this tree.

When the attendant arrived, Suleiman gave him the name and surname. The attendant said that they had wanted to allocate this Suleiman a plot for burial but that his daughter had refused, insisting that he be listed as missing. So he had no headstone. "She comes here every Friday, alone or with her mother. They come here first and then they visit the graves of other martyrs. She comes to my office, too. She asks if anyone has inquired about her father. She always asks this question. There is no shortage of families who are anxious for news of their missing loved ones. So, for their comfort, we give them the bones or limbs of someone else, collected by doctors from the battlefield."

Suleiman's hands were cold and he was breathless. He closed his eyes and thanked the man, before leaving to find his own grave, or perhaps himself. A cold breeze swept between the thick willow leaves. He found his way back to its hanging branches.

He sat there, his legs hugged close to his chest, his chin resting on his kneecaps. The sun had risen high enough to remove the morning shadows from the graves. The smell of rain, the smoke from burning wild rue seed and the occasional sound of prayer filled the air. People slowly gathered around him. He remembered the day they had brought Khurshid home from hospital. Bibi Jan had looked dejected when she learned it was a baby girl. Suleiman, however, was overjoyed. He pressed her to his chest and asked Alia what she had named her. Alia shook her head. He then kissed the baby girl on the face and said, "I will name her myself. She will be Khurshid, her father's sun."

When Khurshid grew up, they would read poems so loudly that Alia would be forced to tell them off. They would hold hands and walk around the pool, surrounded by pots in the garden. "Khurshid Khanum, rise and shine. Say hello to your father, Khurshid Khanum," Suleiman would sing.

Rooted to the spot, he felt his heartbeat slow. He could not believe his eyes. It was her: Alia, Suleiman's own Alia. He could not swallow. He kept blinking in disbelief. Then he collected himself. "You finally came," he thought. It was Alia, accompanied by a girl her size, who wore a headscarf and was smiling. She was walking shoulder-to-shoulder with Alia. It is them. It must be them, Alia and my Khurshid Khanum, he said to himself.

He hid behind the tree, holding his bag to his face to avoid being recognised. She has grown into a lady, he told himself.

Khurshid took something out of her bag – a packet of dates. Her hair was visible under her green headscarf. She was offering the votive dates to the passers-by. She bore an uncanny resemblance to her mother and reminded him of Alia when they had first met.

Khurshid stopped suddenly, as if someone had called her name. A man and a small boy were approaching. Alia took the little boy from the man's arms. Zargham had grown older, into a man, as he would say. His hair had turned grey.

Suleiman was heartbroken and panting. Alia followed the

man. Khurshid left too. Suleiman felt as if he was disintegrating. He fell to the ground. He buried his face in the soft soil under the willow tree and cried loudly. He filled his fists with soil and screamed. He wanted to stop breathing there and then. He wanted his heart to stop pumping blood through his veins. A flood of tears washed his eyes, rolling down his clean-shaven, wrinkled face. He knelt, lifted his head, and hit it against the ground, over and over. He could not lose them.

His knees were wet from his tears. Alia had left. Zargham and the little boy were gone. Someone who looked like Alia seemed to be walking towards the attendant's office. The wind was blowing her skirt. How fast she was walking. It must be Khurshid. She must have a question for the attendant – the same old question.

Suleiman picked up his bag, clenched his fists and headed towards the attendant's room. His steps were slow and his legs shaky. He felt as if he was dragging them behind him. Khurshid waited as the man in the office spoke on the phone. She had not yet asked the question. Suleiman stopped where he was. Tears had washed his entire face. He could not lose Khurshid, and did not want to. He walked faster and more steadily now, edging closer to the girl. He was right behind her, breathing slowly. The attendant ended his call and looked up. The girl asked, "Excuse me, Uncle, has anyone come to ask about my father's grave?" As the attendant began to answer the girl, he kept his gaze fixed on Suleiman.

MY PILLOW'S JOURNEY OF ELEVEN THOUSAND, EIGHT HUNDRED AND SEVENTY-SIX KILOMETRES

Farangis Elyassi

Translated from the Dari by Dr Zubair Popalzai

For many years, I slept comfortably. I always said it was because of my pillow. As soon as I rested my head on that pillow, I fell asleep – so soundly that I only knew 10 p.m. and 6 a.m. on the face of the clock, never the darkness in between those times. It was so difficult for me to leave my pillow each morning and get ready to go to the office. Whenever anyone complained they could not sleep at night, I would reply, "Maybe your pillow is not comfortable – try changing it. I have used the same one for years."

Even my husband would say, "You can fall asleep the moment your head touches the pillow – what kind of skill is that, that I don't have?"

I don't know where my mother bought the pillow all those

years ago, or if she made it herself. It was neither too soft nor too hard for my head. It was just the right size and not too heavy either – exactly right. Yes, I think only my mother could have made me such a balanced pillow.

Things in my country may not have been as convenient or as peaceful as in other countries. There were cuts in the drinking water supply for many hours each day, continuous load-shedding on the power grid and unreliable internet coverage that delayed our work. But our life was beautiful in my beloved homeland. My husband and I had good jobs and a good income. I enjoyed my work: I was a defence lawyer with a foreign organisation, representing poorer clients, mostly women who faced violence at home. I never tired of serving my people and my country. But my husband worried about the growing insecurity. My family would get especially worried about me, because I worked in the courts and attorneys' offices and other judicial buildings. Sudden incidents and explosions meant everyone called their loved ones several times a day to check on them.

Eventually, war and insecurity forced us, like so many others, to leave. My husband made the decision that we should become immigrants. I wasn't happy at all. I kept reminding him of people in our family who could not afford to migrate, who would have no option but to live amid the trouble after we had gone. I didn't want to leave them but I couldn't convince my husband. He believed we would not always have the opportunity to go. There was nothing I could do but accept his decision unwillingly. I started to prepare myself for the journey.

There was a lot to do. I quit my job first, then began to buy essentials to take with me: light summer clothes and winter socks and jackets, household utensils, spices for rice, ground ginger, ghora-e angoor. Friends had told us these things were hard to find abroad and if you did find them they were very expensive. Because my load was so heavy, and the essentials were so many, and the journey was so long, I couldn't take my pillow. I had to be mindful of everything I was carrying, to make sure I didn't exceed my baggage allowance.

Finally, the day to leave arrived. Nervously, I left my homeland for a country many people dream of going to: the United States of America. After we had landed, as we were making our way through the airport, I heard an announcement for people with food items in their luggage. The voice said that if you were carrying unground spices, you should come to a particular desk and inform the authorities. I hoped they would not ask about ground spices. I thought I would quickly collect my luggage and hope for the best.

After a two-day journey, coming off the plane, breathing fresh air and walking on the ground, I felt like a new person. There were clean roads along the river, skyscrapers and houses that looked like cottages. Lush green hills and small rivers made a beautiful picture, but it was quiet everywhere. On the way from the airport, I could only see cars, no humans.

It looked to me like a city of cars. There was not a soul to be seen.

After some time, when we had settled in, I would have my breakfast each morning, clean the house, then sit looking out at the park next to us. With a cup of tea in hand, I would browse the internet in search of a job. I was always busy – with housework, with looking for a job, with preparing for an interview. But I couldn't forget my pillow, because I had not slept well since I arrived in this country.

Over time, I got to know the neighbours. You see each other every day and eventually you have to say hello. I asked them about where I might buy a comfortable pillow. I followed their advice and finally managed to buy myself a new one from a store that specialised in beds, chairs, mattresses and pillows. It seemed very similar to my old pillow, so I was sure my sleep would improve.

That night, when I rested my head on the new pillow, it was so uncomfortable and annoying that I could not sleep at all. I went to exchange it the next morning, but the next night it was the same. I tried several in one week, hoping to find a pillow like my old one, but each night my sleep was worse. Eventually, I got tired of trying. I said to myself, My beloved old pillow, I slept so well on it. Sleep left my eyes the day I left it. I wish I had brought it with me.

For a whole year in a strange country I slept without my pillow. Perhaps I should say I stayed awake for a year without my pillow. At night I would remember happy days back in my country and wonder if it would ever be possible to have that feeling here. Sometimes I would lie awake worrying about the safety of my family back home. I vowed that the next time I visited my country, I would bring my pillow back with me, regardless of the baggage allowance.

At last, my husband and I decided to return to our country, to visit our family for a short time. Oh my God! I had so many preparations to make and gifts to buy for our friends and relatives. For my mother, I chose the small colourful handbags she likes, a watch for my brother, nice clothes for my sisters, toys for the children and delicious chocolates for everyone. After all, I was returning for the first time. "And this time I will come back with my pillow!" Seeing my excitement, the new friends we had made said, "You will not enjoy your country this time because you have grown accustomed to the amenities and comfort of your life here. You will be sad to lose this lifestyle." I said nothing, I just smiled.

Eventually, I returned to my dear homeland. Seeing everyone who had come to the airport to greet us made me so happy. I did not feel tired at all, despite the long journey. At home, my beloved family had prepared ashak, qabooli and bolani. Eating these dishes together added to their flavour; it was a long time since I had eaten with so many people at the same time. I enjoyed the sound of laughter and the noise the children made. Finally, I was rescued from the long silence of America.

My country was the same as I had left it: destroyed but

beautiful, with helpless and poor people, but my own people. And the most beautiful thing was my pillow! That first night, I laid my head on it and slept comfortably after a year. I told my husband, "Didn't I tell you that my pillow was the reason I could not sleep? See how well I can fall asleep now? I don't need any medication."

I was joyful amid the hospitality of our loved ones. Visiting the old markets with my mother, brother and sisters, bargaining with shopkeepers again, eating shor nakhod on broken roads and talking to my people was more relaxing for me than any other comfort or convenience. Two months passed for me like two days, and it was time to say goodbye again.

Once again, I got busy collecting my belongings. Our relatives brought many gifts for us, but this time I was not going to leave behind my pillow. I put it in the biggest suitcase I had.

Again with tears in my eyes and a heart full of loneliness I said goodbye to my homeland and my relatives, to become a traveller again. This time, however, I knew I had my pillow with me. Despite the pain of leaving family and friends, I was certain that I would not have to lie wide-eyed through dark nights. The loneliness would last, but I would not have to bear sleeplessness.

As soon as I landed at the airport in America, I remembered the cheerless days I had spent here before. Here were loneliness and silence again: the city was no longer beautiful to me, neither its sea front, nor its buildings, its landscapes, its parks and restaurants.

I unpacked my pillow as soon as we arrived home. When I put my head down on it that night, it felt a little hard and uncomfortable. I thought it must have been affected by being in a suitcase for two days; it would gradually return to normal.

Days turned into weeks and weeks into months, but my pillow never got comfortable. It has been a year now and I still spend the nights with my eyes wide open. Every night before going to bed, I take sleeping pills, but to no avail; I don't even blink with sleep. Whenever I wake and look at my phone clock, I think: It is still only one o'clock at night, when will it be morning? I keep looking at the clock. Two o'clock, three o'clock, four o'clock, five o'clock; I count the hours till the morning light.

My sleep has no plan to return. The pillow that used to be like a sleeping pill for me has turned into a stone. When I put my head on it, it hurts me. I keep fluffing it and flipping it from left to right and right to left all night long. I some-times remove it altogether, then place it under my head again moments later. But this bundle of silk has become like a bag of stones that pains my head all night long. In the morning, my head aches from its hardness.

I have finally accepted that my peaceful sleep was not bound to my pillow: my sleep was bound to the warm embrace of my country, it was bound to visiting my beloved mother, it was bound to the chatter I shared with my sisters, to the friendship and silliness I shared with my brother, to the laughter I enjoyed with my friends. My peaceful sleep was because of the small service I used to do for my country, because of my streets, because of a sense of freedom one can feel only in one's own country.

IV

AJAH

Fatema Khavari

Translated from the Dari by Dr Zubair Popalzai

When the word "Ajah" is used as a person's name, everyone knows that it refers to the woman called Ajah Ayyub. Ajah means "grandmother", but Ajah Ayyub had no children. She was given the title "Ayyub" because – like the Prophet Ayyub who resisted Satan's temptations in the face of God's trials – Ajah's determination saved her village from drowning.

She was descended from the line of Ibrahim, the bull rider, who, a century earlier, rose up against Amir Abdur Rahman Khan's oppressive rule. The amir banished Ibrahim from Daikundi, one of the central provinces in Afghanistan. Ibrahim travelled four hundred kilometres north to Balkh province, on the border of Uzbekistan, and settled in the district of Chimtal.

In spring and summer, the weather in Chimtal is scorching. In autumn and winter it is freezing. It is in this place of extreme weather, at the foot of Shah Alborz mountain, that Ibrahim, Ajah's grandfather, settled.

After Abdur Rahman Khan died, his son, Prince Habibullah, sought to make amends for his father's injustices. He gave land to all those whom his father had exiled. That was how Ibrahim's two sons, Alidad and Muhammad Ali, became landowners after the death of their father, Ibrahim.

Ajah was Muhammad Ali's daughter. She was born in 1905, a pale-skinned child with dark brown eyes and hair, and a small, determined mouth. She was about seven years old when tuberculosis broke out in the district. Ajah's uncle and his wife perished immediately from the disease.

People began to avoid each other for fear of contracting the sickness. When Ajah's parents also fell ill, she had only the imam of the mosque to help her care for them.

Griefstricken after her parents died, the child visited their graves at the end of every week. She would stand at their graveside, silent and alone, oblivious to the heat or cold until the imam came to fetch her. He took care of Ajah for two years.

One morning the imam took Ajah to survey the land that now belonged to her. Most of it was covered in weeds. The villagers had let their cattle graze there.

"I'm too old to help you farm this land." The imam sounded sad. "I can try to sell it for you . . ."

Ajah shook her head. She looked into the old man's face. "Are you too old to help me plant an orchard?"

The imam rested a hand on Ajah's head and smiled down at her. "An orchard is a good idea. The trees will grow with you. They will be bearing fruits by the time you become a woman. You're a very clever girl; you know what you want and you think ahead. It is your gift."

It was a stormy winter's day with waist-level snow piling up outside when the imam died. By then Ajah knew what it meant to live with grief and she bore the pain of her loss without a word. She had learned to love the imam. He'd rescued her when she was left an orphan, and was the only one in the village who was brave enough to help her bury her parents when they died from tuberculosis.

"You're the daughter I never had," he had told her once. "God did not bless my wife and me with children."

Sha Hussain, the village chief, who had three wives and nine sons, took in the nine-year-old. He would buy her clothes and toys and trinkets and take her everywhere with him. It was probably because he had no daughter that he loved Ajah so much. Eventually, his wives became jealous of the affection he showed the girl. They were too resentful to obey the chief's instructions to treat Ajah as their own daughter.

They forced her to knead the dough for the baking. She milked the cows and cooked for the entire household. She also looked after the three women's nine sons. Yet Ajah never complained.

One afternoon Sha Hussain asked Ajah to bring him tea.

When she placed the tray before him, he noticed her hands were chapped and red with blisters.

"What's happened to your hands?" he asked.

Ajah did not answer.

The village chief got up and led the girl out to the women. He took her hands in his and raised them. "Why are her hands like this? What work have you been giving her?"

"She does nothing but play and sleep," one of the wives replied.

Sha Hussain looked down at the girl. "Is that so?"

Ajah remained silent. The chief let her leave, but he was not satisfied.

Early next morning, he made his way to the kitchen. Ajah was in there, struggling to knead one sair of dough – that was seven kilos! He marched over to the girl, placed a hand on her shoulder, led her out to the courtyard and called his wives.

The women hurried into the courtyard to face a livid husband. "If you are forcing this child to make bread single-handedly for a family of thirteen, then you are no use to me. I'm divorcing you all this very day."

Hearing the word "divorce", the women panicked and began to wail. Ajah tugged at the chief's shirt and knelt before him. "I asked them to give me work because I had nothing to do."

Sha Hussain knew that Ajah was trying to protect his wives. He shook his head at the women. "Don't you have a conscience? How could you ask this child to do the work of all three of you?"

Everything seemed fine after this but the chief knew the resentment of his wives would get worse as time passed so as soon as Ajah turned twelve he wed her to Hakim, Mirza's son.

Mirza, a literate man, had already married off his five daughters. Hakim was his only son.

Ajah learned midwifery from her mother-in-law, Humaira – the only person in the village who delivered children. Whenever a woman was about to give birth, they would call on Humaira at any hour of day or night. Ajah sometimes accompanied her to help.

Humaira desperately wanted grandchildren. She worried when she saw that Ajah was not conceiving. "When will you have a baby?" she chided her. "What's wrong with you? I deliver other people's children day and night and my own son's wife has not yet given him an heir. He's all I have. If you don't conceive, I will find him another wife."

"Where can I get a baby from if God is not giving me one?" Ajah said.

"Well, I'm not going to wait until God gives you a child. I will take another wife for Hakim if it continues like this. Understand?"

It upset Ajah to see other women having babies so easily, and when two years passed without her conceiving, her mother-in-law took another wife called Leila for her son.

Leila was very beautiful. Hakim now spent most of his time talking and laughing with his new wife. Sometimes Ajah heard them from her room and would weep into her pillow at night.

Not a day went by without Leila taunting her about her infertility but Ajah never argued or answered back. Three years passed and Hakim's second wife did not conceive. Now they knew the problem was with Mirza's son. His mother, Humaira, could not bear the taunting and humiliation. She took ill and, soon after, died.

Within the first year of Humaira's death, Hakim decided to go to the mountainous district of Charkent for treatment. There was a traditional healer there who was believed to have the cure for every ailment. He left home one morning to visit the healer and was brought back paralysed from the shoulders down. He'd slipped off the narrow mountain trail, fallen down a cliff and had broken his neck.

When Leila saw there was no hope of him ever fathering children, she gathered the villagers, demanded a divorce in their presence, and left.

Mirza turned to Ajah, his voice soft with sadness. "My son is of no use to you either. Don't waste your life with him. If you want a divorce, I won't stand in your way. Go get married and have children. You are still young."

"No," Ajah said. She stood up straight and pulled her shoulders back. "I do not want another husband. Besides, you're my family; you're all I have. Who abandons their family in difficult times?"

Ajah cared for Hakim for seven years until he died. Again Mirza told her that she should remarry.

"I'm too old for that now," she said. She was just twenty-seven, but her hair had gone grey at the front. Now, children called her Ajah, or Grandmother. She did not mind that; in fact, it pleased her very much. Soon, everyone referred to her by that name.

Mirza divided his wealth among his children and gave Hakim's share to Ajah. She planted more trees on the hectares of land she had inherited. She filled her orchard with every variety of fruit tree in the province. Her almonds, peaches, nectarines and apples grew fat on their branches, and alongside them she grew all kinds of berries, black and red and white. Ajah's orchard became famous throughout Balkh province. It could be clearly seen from the very top of Shah Alborz mountain.

In July 1940, around the time that the government had announced that every able-bodied man must serve in the army, an earthquake struck the district. The village had almost been emptied of men. Children, old men and the women had been left to tend to the animals and farm the land. It was a terrible time for everyone.

Her orchard was not destroyed but many of her fruit trees were damaged. Her beloved walnuts now stood with their roots exposed. She had wanted to grow old with them.

Later that month Ajah travelled to Shah Alborz to collect badrah. Every year, she would climb its slopes to harvest the medicinal plant. She had come to know the entire Alborz area like the back of her hand.

She was halfway up the mountain when she paused to look down on her orchard. It was then that she saw that the earthquake had split the slopes. A fissure now ran all the way down from the foot of the mountain to her village. She realised immediately what would happen to her beloved orchard when the melting snow turned to water and flowed into the ravine created by the earthquake. That water would go straight down to their village and destroy their crops and homes.

On her return, she called everyone to her house and pointed at the long gully that the earthquake had made from the mountain to the north side of the village. It was just visible from where they stood.

"Look up there," she said pointing towards the slope. "Imagine what will happen when the snow melts and the water runs off the slopes into that gully."

"What are you talking about?" asked Khalil, the village chief.

"That gully," Ajah said, "will direct a flood straight towards the village."

"Are you out of your mind, Ajah? What flood? My hair turned grey here and I do not remember the village flooding even once."

"The bottom of the mountain is not like before! I saw it myself when I went up Shah Alborz to collect badrah. If you think me a fool and don't believe me, go and see for yourself."

Khalil irritated her. He was so different from Sha Hussain, who had been kind to her when she was a child.

"So, what do you suggest we do now?" the old man said with a sneer.

"We should dig a diversion channel to redirect the water and prevent the flood from entering the village."

"But who will dig the channel? There are no men left. The government enlisted them all. Do you think these kids and old men should pick up shovels and pickaxes and dig?"

"But the women are still here. We will do the digging."

"And who will work in the farm, look after the kids and cook?"

"We will take turns."

"Ajah, you're uttering nonsense. Can these women pick up shovels and pickaxes and dig the ground?"

"Of course they can! You just said they work the farm and look after the children. Why then can't they use a pickaxe and a shovel to dig a swale?"

"It's men's work, Ajah Ayyub."

"Is it?" Ajah adjusted her scarf and returned to her house.

The next day she made her way to the north end of the village where the gully reached her orchard. She started digging, ignoring Khalil's sneers and jibes. She pretended not to hear the women who joked among themselves that she had grown old and had therefore lost her senses.

Ajah dug for a month until she connected her swale to the river.

The heavy rains began falling in November. One day it rained all afternoon, then late into the night. They were in bed when the water struck the village. Walls and houses crumbled under the weight of the tumbling flood. Women and children were washed away along with the livestock. Only Ajah's house and orchard stood untouched.

A couple of days later, the weather was still brooding. The dawn light filtered through the hole in the ceiling of the room. All the houses in the village were made of mud, with semi-circular ceilings. In the dim light Ajah Ayyub stood before a large square mirror with grass stalks beautifully etched around its edges. She combed her hair and noticed that she had many more grey strands at the front of her head than at the back. She divided her hair into two equal parts, brought them to the front and started braiding them. When she finished, she flipped them back behind her head.

She had a beautiful araqchin hat woven in green and yellow. She put it on, her grey hair still showing, covered the hat with her red floral linen scarf and left the room. The chickens had come out and were strutting in the courtyard, pecking at everything.

Ajah went to the kitchen, picked up two pateer breads

from the tablecloth, poured water into a jar and tied a piece of leather around the head of the vessel. She put them both on the patio before entering the wheat storage room. Ajah returned with a shovel and a pickaxe and placed them next to the water and the bread. Then she brought out the donkey from her barn, secured the items from the patio in her saddlebag and laid it on the animal's back.

The village was still asleep when she walked down the alley. She looked at the walls of the houses on either side, damaged by the floodwater, and sighed. Some of the trees were partially uprooted. In the dim light of the early morning, the farmlands lay flat and empty. Everything had been washed away. Ajah headed for the mountain, guiding the animal with caution because the path had become a mud track.

Ajah dismounted at the foot of the mountain and measured with her eyes the distance between the village and where she stood. She lifted the saddlebag off the donkey and picked up her shovel and pickaxe. Tightening her scarf around her head, she rolled up her sleeves and walked towards the end of the slope. Ajah began to dig.

She returned home late at night when the village was asleep, and rose with the morning call to prayer. Ajah packed her donkey with her tools, along with a small meal of bolani, and headed for the mountain.

A few days later, the villagers noticed Ajah's absence.

"What's happened to Ajah Ayyub? Where is she?"

"We saw her at the base of Shah Alborz," Shabir, a young shepherd replied. "She's been up there for a couple of days."

"What's she doing there?" the women asked.

"Digging," the boy replied.

"Digging what?"

"A big drain."

They remembered the flood that had done so much damage to the village, sparing only Ajah's orchard and her house.

"Maybe she's right," Fazila, Shabir's mother, said.

When Ajah arrived home, several women were sitting on her patio. She greeted them and tied the donkey.

"We hardly see you these days," Shabir's mother said.

Ajah seated herself among them. "I go to the mountain every day. I have work to do."

Fazila put a cup of tea in Ajah's hand. "I will join you tomorrow."

Ajah shook her head. "No. You have to plough the land. I know what to do."

"You are just one woman. How can you dig such a big drain on your own?" Fazila said.

Ajah did not answer her. She looked around her kitchen. The women had tidied it. They'd also prepared food and tea for her and left them on her stove.

Ajah set out earlier than usual the next morning. She was busy working when she heard voices. She turned and saw that Fazila and two other siah sar had come along with their cattle.

There was no sign of their sons whose job it was to tend to the animals. "Where are the boys?" Ajah asked.

"We left them to plough the land," one of the women replied. "We appointed the elderly men to teach them."

The women left the animals to graze and, pickaxe in hand, they placed themselves behind Ajah and started digging.

By the second week, fifteen more women had come to join them. By then, they'd managed to widen the channel, and it was now many times longer than when they'd started. At lunchtime they spread a big cloth on the ground on which they laid yoghurt, chakka, roghan-e zard and boiled eggs. They sat around the food and chatted and laughed while they ate.

Fazila went quiet for a while. She was staring at the work they'd just completed. "How much have we dug so far, Ajah?"

"About six hundred metres," Ajah said.

"We did all this!" Fazila said. Her eyes were wide with disbelief.

"We all did this! Old Khalil said we couldn't," Ajah laughed. "I would like to see his face when it is finished."

She loosened her scarf and smiled at the group. "Imagine how much more we can do together."

It was mid-November when the heavy rains began again. Aware that they had not completed the digging, Ajah saw the dark clouds gathering and ordered her companions to hurry back to the village because the downpour would not stop anytime soon. They grabbed their tools, loaded them onto the donkey, herded their cattle and hurried back to the village.

"Will all our hard work pay off?" The woman who spoke sounded worried.

"We must wait and see what happens," Ajah replied calmly.

It was early afternoon when they arrived in the village. The rain had got heavier and the flooding had already started. They watched the thundering water sweep down through the channel they had cut, diverting part of the flow towards their agricultural lands. Their channel was not enough to turn away all the water, but most of it was redirected towards the river. So forceful was the flow, both sides of the channel were eroded, making it wider.

After the flood, almost every woman in the village joined the digging. They divided the work and took turns. Some stayed behind to look after the cattle and the children and cook for everyone, while others accompanied Ajah, who was there every day guiding them.

They were driven on by the outcome of the most recent flood. And in a couple of months, they had completed the excavation so that when the next great downpour came, they watched and celebrated as the rushing water, contained by the swale, missed the village completely and spilled into the river.

More floods came, and each time the water flowed straight into the river.

When the men returned to the village, they were astonished to see the women's work.

They could not believe that Ajah and the women had built such a huge diversion channel by themselves.

"And why not?" Ajah said, with a quiet challenge in her voice. "They till the land; they raise your children. They lift buckets of water from the well every day. How difficult is digging a tiny channel when we women come together?"

THE RED BOOTS

Naeema Ghani

*Translated from the Pashto by Shekiba Habib
and Zarghuna Kargar*

It doesn't matter what colour your boots are – they could be red or black or blue. Or maybe for you it's a dress or a notepad or an umbrella that you chose. The important thing is that you chose. And I chose a pair of boots.

I was about eight or nine. I heard my mother saying to my father, "This girl doesn't have any shoes for the winter. Yesterday, I noticed that the ones she has are torn." I hadn't realised that my shoes were ripped – I didn't like them anyway. They were very stiff and hurt my feet.

My father looked at me. He said, "OK, my daughter, tomorrow we'll go and get you a good pair of boots so you can be nice and warm in the winter." My father often said things like this, especially when we were sad: he would promise to buy us new clothes and shoes. But we knew there wasn't much money in our family for buying new things and that he was just trying to cheer us up.

Sometimes for Eid, or at the start of a new school year, we would get something new. When he did buy us shoes, my father would usually try to choose a pair we could wear in both warm weather and cold. And we were five sisters in all, so our clothes were handed down from one to the next until they were quite worn out. But this time I felt that my father really would buy me new shoes. For one thing, my mother had asked him to and, for another, I wasn't sad. So it couldn't have been just to console me that he said he would buy me new boots.

I already knew that this winter I would be wearing the blue jacket my sister Farida had outgrown. My mother had told me this and had added, "I'll ask your father to buy you a new pair of shoes and you won't need anything else for the winter." I didn't care that much about clothes, so this was fine by me.

The next day, true to his word, my father took me shopping. We walked very slowly towards the bazaar. My father was a strong, broad-shouldered man. He always wore a white shalwar kameez with a black and white blazer. He'd broken his leg when he was young and it had been treated with traditional medicines, but the bone had healed in a curve. He limped when he walked and for me this made him special. It meant I could always recognise him in a crowd of other men. I wouldn't lose him, walking in the bazaar.

Every time we had to buy something, we would come to

this very same market. My father had many friends here. I'm not sure if it was just my impression but it seemed to me that most of the shopkeepers in this bazaar were elderly men. Or perhaps my father avoided younger shopkeepers. We went into the shops, and they would talk to him at length. Sometimes they talked about prices, sometimes about the crowd that day. Sometimes they shook their heads together over this new generation that was so demanding.

It was a busy place, the second-hand market, made up of single- and two-storey mud structures. The shops were old and you could smell them as you approached. Damp mixed with shoe leather – a smell that was annoying and particular at the same time. In bellowing voices, vendors promised cheap prices and quality that couldn't be found anywhere else, whether they were selling sandals, laces, wax and brushes, or enticing shoppers to taste their bolani and chickpeas. Walking past, you had to manoeuvre round carts heaped with plastic shoes. Cars hooted as they inched forward though the crowd, their horns chiming with the cacophony of calls to buy.

My father walked ahead, and I a few steps behind him. We had visited a number of shops already. I was tired and didn't think we'd find anything suitable in this bazaar. It seemed that my father had brought me here just so he could talk to his friends.

We entered one more shop. This one was under the stairs and we had to bend down to enter. I looked around despondently. The shoes here were very old and faded. Then my eye was drawn to a pair of red boots hanging from a nail on the wall. I'd seen plastic boots in different shades, but it was the first time I'd seen coloured boots in leather. The boots were second-hand, and stuffed with old cloth to give them shape, but they were beautiful. The leather was red and shiny; the shafts were made of red suede, with metal studs. They would reach my shins, I thought. I was captivated.

I immediately imagined what Farida's reaction would be if I came home with these boots. And then, if I wore them in the morning and stood in front of our block of flats, all the other girls would be excited too. I imagined the faces of each of my friends. I thought I had found something no one else could find, however hard they tried. That is the special thing about second-hand goods: you can search the whole bazaar and never find a match.

I gestured to my father that I wanted those boots. He gave them a quick glance and dismissed them. "My daughter, let's go to another shop." But I knew my father. If I insisted, he'd pay attention. I said emphatically, "Aba, no! Those boots are fine."

The shopkeeper looked from me to my father. My dad nodded, reluctantly. "Brother, can you hand us those red boots?"

Sometimes grown-ups are too sensible. They only want undamaged goods and those that serve their intended purpose. For them, a cardboard box is for storing things and it takes a child to show them that a cardboard box is good for playing in, or making a toy car out of, or turning into a house for dolls or toy animals. For a grown-up, winter boots should be comfortable and warm. But if they listened to their children, they would realise that other things are important: that boots are great for sliding on snow, or perfect for showing off to friends.

The elderly shopkeeper reached with his shaky, wrinkled hands and pulled the cloth stuffing out of the boots before handing them to my father. They were old, their soles worn so smooth it would make walking on the snow almost impossible. My dad examined them and measured them against his palm. He paused, then he said, "My daughter, these will not last you to the end of winter." I didn't reply, so he told me to try them on.

When I put them on, they looked bright and shiny, and it was the first time I'd ever felt I had something beautiful. They came up to my shins.

My father asked, "How are they? Do they fit you?"

I didn't know if they were the right size at all but I knew I wanted them. I could only look at my feet. I didn't say anything. My father knelt and pressed the pointed toe cap of the boot. He shook his head. "No, they feel tight around your toes, I don't think they're the right size. They'll only hurt your feet." He said, more gruffly: "Let's go to another shop."

While I'd been trying them on, the shopkeeper hadn't stopped talking. He said we'd never find anything of the same quality in the whole bazaar, that he would reduce the price for us, and that when a person bought something from him, they remained his customer forever.

I took the boots off and handed them to my father. He passed them to the shopkeeper, who tried a softer approach. "Didn't you like them?"

"You can see they are too small for my daughter," my father replied.

"But brother, these boots are so nice and soft. You can see the child loves them. Buy them for her."

My father pretended he didn't hear. He took me by the hand and made for the door, saying to the shopkeeper: "She's a child – by the middle of winter, she'll want another pair. These boots are not her size, and aren't meant for winter."

I said, "Aba, they fit me fine, they didn't hurt my feet."

I could see the irritation in my father's eyes. We came out of the mud hut but I left my heart inside with the red boots.

My father took me to many other shops but I refused to try on anything else. He tried to convince me of the virtues of other pairs of boots. He even asked the shopkeepers to help him with their patter, but I wouldn't budge. I wasn't going to accept defeat. It was past midday and we were still walking around the bazaar. My father gave me a long look.

"OK, tell me what you want to do."

I didn't hesitate. "I want those red boots."

Again, my father walked ahead, and I followed him back

to the shop. The shopkeeper seemed to be waiting for us. "I told you that the girl likes these boots." My father frowned in response. He helped me put the boots on again and repeated that they were not my size and that I'd suffer all winter. I just kept looking happily at my feet from every angle, and this was how my father knew I wouldn't change my mind. I had my moment of triumph: he bought me the boots and I carried them proudly out of the shop.

When we got home, my sister Farida was the first to look inside the bag. She ran up to my father. "Aba, Aba, you must buy me the same boots!"

Farida was ahead of me in everything. She was good at maths, she was even good at shopping – she had good taste. She made wooden dolls with beautiful clothes. Everyone liked Farida: our teachers did, our neighbours did. I thought even her name was prettier than mine. This was the first time I had had something better, something I had chosen.

My father replied wearily: "OK, I will take you shopping next time, but bring me a glass of water. She was so stubborn – she made me buy her those." I was sure that even if they combed the bazaar, my sister wouldn't find a pair of boots like mine. I told Farida so, confidently. I would be the only girl to have such nice boots that winter.

The night passed slowly, as it always does for someone waiting for a good thing to come in the morning. I woke at dawn; unusually early for me. I had breakfast and got dressed.

I put on my red boots and tucked my partoog bottoms inside them, so that the whole of each boot could be seen.

When I went outside, no one noticed me at first. I wasn't sure how to get the others' attention. I decided that instead of going up to my friends, I would stand proudly by the wall, pretending to be upset. This caught the girls' attention – first they saw me and then they saw my boots. One by one, they came towards me saying, "Wow! Wow!" They gathered around me and I tried to act normal.

"Your boots are very beautiful!"

"Are they new?"

"Yes, I went out with my father yesterday to buy them."

I started calmly, but then I told them the whole story: how my father hadn't wanted to buy these boots but I had insisted. The whole day became about my boots. But their story didn't end here; there was to be more of it. By evening, my toes were hurting. The next morning, I had trouble putting the boots on. My feet seemed to have swollen. With the greatest difficulty, I pulled them on and tried walking. I felt like my toes and heels were burning.

School closed for winter break. This was our time to play games but it was hard to focus on winning when I was constantly distracted by the pain in my feet. I wanted to write on the walls that the winner of the game is the person whose feet are comfortable!

Because I lagged behind, girls started to refuse to have me on their teams. But I couldn't do anything about it: I didn't want to admit that the reason I couldn't run fast was that my famous red boots hurt my feet. Even walking was difficult: I would have to take small, slow steps. One day, when I was playing a game of hopscotch with my friends, I had to stop suddenly and forfeit my turn. I sat in a corner of the yard and took my boots off. My feet had blistered.

It wasn't even easy getting the boots on and off. I had to stamp on the floor to get my feet in and tug relentlessly to get them out. The situation got worse when I jumped into a puddle one day and got water inside my boots. When they dried, they were even tighter than before. I didn't say a word to anyone. Only God and I knew how much trouble those boots were causing me.

My favourite of all our games was sliding on the snow. One person would run along the snow, their arms stretched back to hold the hands of another person, crouched and ready to slide in their wake. If you're at the back, you just put your feet together and let them pull you along. But even in this game I fell over, because the worn soles of my boots were so slippery that I couldn't keep my balance.

Winter slowly ended and a new school year approached. The weather was warming up and eventually the season of my red boots would end. I didn't want to let them go. They would barely last a moment longer, but I loved them as much as when my father had first bought them for me. At school, we were getting ready for the usual beginning-of-year celebrations.

We practised reciting poems and hoped we would be chosen to perform at the festival, in front of all our teachers and families and friends.

This year, I was on the list, along with some of my friends, to perform in a choir made up of students from different years. We were twenty in all and every day we practised our song. We already knew it by heart: the blue sky song. We had to stand in lines, grouped by height. Our teachers wanted us to look neat and well organised.

On the day of the festival, I woke early again. I put on my black uniform and wrapped my white scarf around my head. I pulled on my red boots and went to school.

The schoolyard was crowded, everyone seemed to be rushing. We were all worried that we had forgotten something we needed for the festival. Some students were going over their lines, sure they'd forget them. Some were exercising their voices, worried they wouldn't hold steady for the show. Others were fixing their hair or fretting about their clothes.

The festival began and we all stood ready. Our choir would be performing last.

Suddenly an older girl spotted my boots. I hadn't noticed her before – she was tall, with ginger hair tied up in a ponytail. She stood up and said, "Hey! We are all wearing the same sort of shoes and you're wearing red boots! We're all supposed to look the same!"

She caught the ear of the teacher in charge. The teacher was now looking in our direction and seemed to be studying us. "Don't talk so loud!" I hissed. "The teacher heard you, don't get me taken out of the group!" I looked helplessly at a friend of mine. My friend said, "Don't worry, we have time. Go and switch shoes with another girl."

This was common practice. Girls and boys would exchange shoes all the time at our school, especially for playing sport, as trainers were expensive and this was the only way we'd have enough pairs to go around. I could easily have asked someone to swap, but I hesitated. It was different this time. How could I give someone else my boots to wear: the red boots only I had, the ones I'd chosen myself? I decided that, even if I had to forfeit my place in the choir, I wouldn't exchange my boots with anyone.

The time came for us to go up on stage and take our designated spots. I felt nervous as I walked up. I kept looking at the teacher, expecting her to take me by the hand and walk me out of the group. And so it happened: the teacher put her hand on my shoulder and said, "Stay here."

I resigned myself to losing my place. But the teacher smiled. She gave me the microphone and said: "Take this and stand in front of the group." I did as she told me but when I looked back, I saw everyone else standing on their spots, while I stood alone out front. The teacher took me by the shoulders and turned me to face the audience. That was how I became the leader of the choir.

The song began. As the whole school looked on, I stood proudly in the red leather boots I had chosen, singing to celebrate the beginning of the new year.

BLOSSOM

Zainab Akhlaqi

Translated from the Dari by Dr Negeen Kargar

I remember us sitting under our apple tree before the school day started, laughing at the minister for education. We were drinking green tea and sitting with pens and paper, preparing for our protest. We needed to choose our slogans. I suggested: "Wake Up, Minister! Where Are Our Teachers and Books?"

But Shaherbano laughed at me. So I said, "What about 'The Minister Is So Incompetent He Can't Even Keep His Promises!'" I loved my slogans but Shaherbano couldn't stop laughing. She wiped her running eyes with the corner of her white headscarf.

"Nekbakht, say something good, don't ruffle the minister's feathers."

"When the headmistress gave you permission to hold the protest, did she say we had to please the minister?" I retorted.

"The point is to get his attention so he does what we want."

Finally, we decided to write: "Dear Minister, We Want Teachers! Dear Minister, We Want Books!" Between ourselves, we also said a lot of other things to the minister but we didn't write those down. Shaherbano said, "If I become minister for education, I won't let any girl be uneducated." I laughed again, but when I looked across at Shaherbano, I saw she was no longer laughing with me. I said to her, more seriously, "But Shaherbano, you are daydreaming! When we finish school next year, for us that will be the end of studying: how can you become minister for education?"

Shaherbano looked away from me at the flowers in the garden. She said, "Remember these blossoms. I am telling you now that one day I will be minister for education and I will go from door to door, telling families to let their daughters go to school. When those little girls follow me, I will give them notebooks and pens. I will give them notebooks and pens to last them until they can finish a PhD."

"Are you saying you're fed up with sharing your pen and notebooks with me?" I teased her.

She smiled. "You never stop fooling around."

I heard my mother call out fiercely that I needed to come quickly and finish the carpet. Most days I missed school because I had to help weave the carpets my parents sold. I made a face. "Dear Minister, I have to go. Or she'll shout that I can't go to school and I have to marry the shepherd."

"Your mother didn't listen to my mother, did she?" Shaherbano replied.

"What can I say? All they care about is what people will say: one ear stuck to the wall and the other stuck to the door."

"Can't you try to explain?"

"What's the point? They don't want me to marry now, but they like to discuss it when they run out of money."

"I wish there was something I could do."

"My lovely friend, the only reason I still come to school is because of you."

It was true. Whenever I felt down and didn't go to school, Shaherbano would come like an angel to rescue me and draw me out, like a car stuck in the mud. The idea of a protest had come to her while she was trying to help me.

That's how it all began: I had missed school one day after a family had come to ask my parents for my hand. Shaherbano came to see me after school. She saw my eyes, red and puffy, and scolded me. "Why are you crying instead of coming to school? You know we had history and geography today!"

I cut her off. "I don't care about history and geography – especially Afghanistan's geography. It's just made of war and cruelty, fighting and Taliban. I wish I had been born in another geography!"

Shaherbano was angry. She said, "It's because our people are illiterate. Even many of our kings and ministers were illiterate: they could only fight, not read or write. And people danced to the drum of their ignorance. Now they say the Taliban has changed, but how could they change without reading a book? If a person never reads a book, how can he change? If all our parents were literate, girls like you wouldn't face these troubles. Our geography itself would not be in such constant danger. Nekbakht, our history must change at some point."

Deep in my heart, I believed every bit of her speech. I wanted things to change, but I always felt small compared to my problems. I was silent.

Shaherbano looked at me. "Who was it this time?"

"My parents want me to marry the shepherd Khudadad."

"You are not married yet, he only came to ask for your hand. If you finish your studies, maybe you can change your parents' minds. I will tell my mother to speak to your mother."

I took a deep breath and hugged her. I said to her, "My dear sister, what would I do without you?" And I really meant it.

I told her my father wanted to beat me when I said I wouldn't marry his cousin Khudadad because he smelled of sheep. I reminded her how, when we asked our chemistry teacher what love is, he had thought for a long time. Then he said, "Love is an element. Whatever you see and like, that is love."

Shaherbano asked me, "What is your love, Nekbakht?"

I said, "All I know is that my love is not Khudadad!"

We both burst out laughing.

Shaherbano stayed at my house and reviewed the day's

lessons with me. She did this often. Sometimes she'd deliberately leave her books with me so that I couldn't miss school the next day.

But again and again, our teacher was absent. Each time, our headmistress would warn us that no teacher would be present the next day. I said to Shaherbano, "I don't think there is unbroken studying in my destiny." She took my hand forcefully and led me to the headmistress's office.

"What are you doing?"

"Come with me, you will find out."

When we entered the office, the headmistress was busy leafing through pages in a folder. She looked up kindly. "Tell me, my dears, what do you want to say?" Shaherbano asked if we could stage a protest to demand teachers and books. The headmistress took her glasses off to see us better. She smiled. "You can, and I hope you succeed," she told us.

Shaherbano was excited and assured her we would. I didn't say anything until we had left the office, then I scolded Shaherbano for attempting the impossible. "How can we do this?!" Once again, Shaherbano convinced me with one of her speeches and I felt ashamed of my fearfulness. That's how we came to be sitting under the apple tree, coining slogans to put to the minister for education.

After we had made our posters, we took them to a printing shop and made some copies to hand out to the girls in other classes too. The headmistress helped us get police permission for our protest and instructed the school's security guards to support us. She found journalists to come to our forgotten corner of Kabul and cover our protest. They would need to find their way there anyway, but no one knew yet what was coming.

I knew that my parents would never allow me to protest, so I did not ask their permission. Shaherbano's determination had infected me too. If they beat me, they beat me – they couldn't kill me. I joined Shaherbano on the street. When I was in the middle of the road, stopping the traffic from moving, I felt that, instead of blood, divine power was coursing through my veins. I felt my body gripped with happiness as we shouted our demands for books and teachers.

Every time we shouted, people looked at us – because our voices came from our hearts, filled with our little sorrows and the dust of life's trouble. In just a few words, we shouted out the hopes of many girls. At that moment, I felt so powerful I believed no one could block my path or rob me of my future.

After an hour of protesting, I sat down with the other girls from Sayed ul-Shuhada high school. Our excitement ebbed as everyone grew tired under the hot sun. When I came home, I found my mother angry. She told me off in every way she knew how; she told me that if a girl is seen on TV no one will marry her. I was tired and did not confront her. I wanted to avoid a beating.

The next day I waited again under the blossoming trees in

our garden till Shaherbano came to ask why I hadn't come to school. I told her that the Khudadad family knew that I had joined the protest and had told my father I shouldn't be allowed to go to school anymore. I said to Shaherbano, "You carry on and become minister for education. That will be a better way to solve the problems of girls like me." I told her she should take my uniform and my school things and use them in my place.

Shaherbano said, "Please don't give up." She even said she would talk to my father if I thought that was a good idea. She told me the police had come to our school that day. She was hopeful it was because of the protest – that they were checking whether we really didn't have books or teachers. She was right, in a way, that our voices had been heard somewhere: soon we wouldn't need either books or teachers.

The next afternoon, I waited again for Shaherbano to come and ask me why I hadn't come to school. But as I lingered under the trees, I heard a deafening noise. Before I could work out what it was, there was another explosion, then another, then gunfire. I stood still while the neighbours talked loudly. They were saying the school had been attacked.

My first thought was of Shaherbano. As I ran towards the school, I said to myself: Don't be crazy, nothing has happened to her. I felt the ground was pulling my legs down. But even from where I was, I could see enormous clouds of dust and smoke. As I got near to the school, I felt suffocated, first by the smoke and dust-filled air, then by the sight of scraps of clothes, metal and flesh. I tried to swallow the pain in my throat so I could get past and enter the school premises. There was blood everywhere I stepped; even the water in the drains ran red.

People surrounded the dead bodies. I could hear loud cries and screams from all around. In a corner, was a heap of bags and books by a half-burnt wall. There was an old sign on the wall. It read "Freshly Dug Well". Yes, a well drilled deep enough to accommodate all the dreams of Afghan schoolgirls. People were collecting the bloodied belongings and remnants of their children. I scanned the books and notebooks, praying that none of Shaherbano's would be there.

I searched everywhere but I found no sign of Shaherbano. Maybe she'd been wounded and taken to hospital. I went to one of the hospitals where they were taking the dead and the injured. There were injured bodies everywhere, and chaos.

There was a row of corpses covered in white cloths. From time to time, a person would uncover each body, looking for the person they were missing. I saw an older man reciting to himself as he lifted each cloth, "My daughter – my Kamila – is OK. She is a good girl. She is fine." But when he reached the last corpse, he fell to the ground. I feared that I also couldn't stand, but I could.

A woman was lying on a bed, holding a small body. In another corner, a young boy was sitting in shock next to a body. I went to him and tried to ask kindly, "Was she your sister?" Through cracked lips, he replied hoarsely: "She is my younger sister."

"Where are your mother and father?"

"I have an injured sister in another hospital – my mother is with her. My father is trying to find my older sister."

Pain squeezed my throat. I felt such hatred for the attackers, I had nothing to console him with. I turned around and, tears flowing, looked over the scene. On one of the hospital walls was a list. As I approached it, I realised that all the names were mixed together: the martyrs, the wounded and the witnesses. I looked through them, one by one, but Shaherbano's name was not there.

I went to another hospital; her name was not there either. I went to a third hospital. Just as I was deciding Shaherbano must be safe, I found her name on a list of martyrs.

I read it several times to make sure it really was my Shaherbano's name, and her father's name. I leaned on a wall and I passed out. When I came to, I remembered what I had just seen and fainted again. I do not know how many times it happened.

But later, I remembered the day Shaherbano asked me, "What is your love, Nekbakht?" Now I knew my love was her and my friendship with her. She had done so much for me; nothing could have stopped her but death. I wasn't going to abandon her dreams now.

My family ate in silence that night. As we sat around the dinner cloth, I played with the potato on my plate. I said, "I am going back to school tomorrow." I watched my mother with one eye and my father with the other. I felt cold sweat running down my back. My mother began to say, helplessly, "Khudadad—" but my father cut her off. "Am I her father or is Khudadad? I say my daughter should go back to school. We don't know how long any of us has. Go, my child, and live the way you want to live."

I was speechless. Shaherbano was right. We had to show some spirit in the face of our struggles. Two days later, I put on my black school uniform and white scarf and filled my bag with notebooks. I cut a fresh branch of blossom from our garden and went to school.

This story is written in honour of Afghan schoolgirls, and in particular the students of Sayed ul-Shuhada high school in Dasht-e-Barchi, Kabul. The story draws on the real events of 8 May 2021, but is a work of fiction.

HASKA'S DECISION

Rana Zurmaty

Translated from the Pashto by Shekiba Habib

The morning sun was soon to rise. Haska was sitting close to the tanoor with a pot of dough. She picked off a bit and rounded it in her hands. She dipped her fingers into a bowl of water and flattened the ball, until she had a full circle. She leaned deep into the clay oven to stick the chapatti to its side.

Wranga came in, rubbing her sleepy eyes with one hand, golden curls falling onto her face.

"Moor Jani!" she called to her mother. "Did Baba bring my biscuit?"

"No, my sweet girl! Your father is on the night shift, he hasn't come home yet. Go back to bed and I will let you know when he gets here."

"No no! I want to sit by you."

"OK, sit then. But don't shout – everyone is asleep."

Haska patted the space beside her. Wranga rested her little

head against her mother's shin, playing with her own hair. Haska thought how little food there would be in the house when her husband came home, tired and hungry: just this bread and tea, after she'd milked the cow. But at least today he would get his salary from the pharmacy and bring home the week's groceries.

Little Wranga was so quiet against her leg, she thought the child had fallen asleep. As she looked down at her daughter, Haska was jolted by a gunshot, too close. Then, another. Wranga jumped into Haska's arms. They heard the birds fleeing the trees outside. Haska clung tightly to Wranga.

"Oh God's mercy! Who have they shot this time?"

The men and women of her husband's family rushed out of their rooms, towards the noise. Haska's mother-in-law knew she wouldn't be able to follow them – her feet wouldn't carry her further than the yard. She told her grandson to fetch her a glass of cold water, then said to her husband, "Please go and find out who they have killed in the village." She signalled to her elder son to leave his wife and children at home and go with his father.

Haska's father-in-law put on his kalaoush and they left the house. Wranga wouldn't let Haska put her down. Carrying the child, she went into her room and stared at the clock hanging on the wall. "It's seven o'clock, why isn't he home yet?" she asked herself. Jamal brought his grandmother her water. Before she had finished drinking it, the men returned, carrying a body into the yard.

The old lady coughed out her sip of water. "Who is this? Why you are bringing him to our house?" Panic rose in her voice.

Haska's father-in-law spread his shawl on the ground to lay the body on. The dead man's blue clothes were stained with blood and his pockets were ripped.

Haska's mother-in-law began to scream. Haska stood fixed to the spot. But Wranga ran up to the body. "Baba! Did you bring me a biscuit?" She pushed on his chest with her tiny hands, trying to make him move. She looked at her mother and said: "He didn't bring biscuits. He lied to me." She kept tapping his chest. "Baba, Baba!"

In a matter of a few minutes, the villagers had gathered. Haska's own mother also arrived. She hugged Haska tight, then tried smacking her on her face to bring her to life. But Haska did not respond. She was standing tall and silent like a Buddha. Finally, her mother gripped her arm and pulled her to Gul Khan's dead body.

Haska knelt. His eyes were closed and his body was bloody. There was a gunshot wound next to his heart. Haska put her hand on it then laid her head on his chest. She couldn't hear anything. She touched his face, kissed him on his forehead and wiped away the bloodstains with her scarf. Tears gathered in her eyes. Suddenly she howled and began slapping her own face.

The women in the yard covered their mouths with their hands, then began saying quietly to each other:

"Oh! She is so brazen, so shameless! She is crying for her husband in front of everyone."

"Oy, oy, oy! This is so bad."

"We haven't seen a woman like this in our village until today."

Haska's mother-in-law gave Haska's mother the eye. Her look said, "Take Haska to her room." Haska's mother touched her daughter's arm. But Haska would not move. She held Gul Khan's hand tightly, saying, "Please don't separate me from him. Please leave me alone." Her mother could not move her, so a few of the other women surrounded Haska and raised her to her feet. They led her to her room. There her mother held her and tried to talk to her.

"My daughter! I feel what is in your heart. But please don't bring shame on us in front of all these people. They will all talk about you. Don't make yourself the tale of every household."

Haska looked at her mother with bloodshot eyes.

"Babo, I have lost everything. Dark night has spread over my bright day and you are telling me not to become the talk of every household."

She leaned her head against the wall and stared at the ceiling. Her lips moved silently, "Oh my Wranga and Jamal, what will happen to them?" She started and rushed out to find her children.

Haska saw that her mother-in-law had brought the children to their father's body. She kept saying to her grandchildren,

"Your baba died. Look at him. This is your last chance, you won't see him again." Haska hurried towards them and held her children tight. Little Wranga wiped Haska's tears with her tiny hands, saying to her, "Tell Baba to get up and bring me a biscuit."

Men came with the kafan and the coffin. Gul Khan was a martyr and didn't need to be washed. They wrapped him in the clothes he had on and put him in the coffin. Four men hoisted it onto their shoulders. Haska and her children ran after them and the women murmured, "Oh! So shameful! So bad!" But none of this affected Haska. It was her world that was ruined, not anybody else's.

Everything came to an end: Gul Khan was buried and Haska became a widow.

Within a fortnight there were enquiries; men from near and far vying for Haska's hand in marriage. She was known for her blue eyes and golden hair. She didn't have any education but Gul Khan had loved her for being clever and kind. They had been through hard times together. Haska knew there were men out there counting the days till she ended her iddat, the period of mourning she had to observe as a widow. Haska imagined them like wild animals waiting to pounce on their prey.

Whenever Haska had a moment to herself, she would go to her room and gaze at Gul Khan's photograph on the wall. Sometimes she would converse so deeply with him that, outside the room, the family would hear her laughing. They thought she was losing her mind. But Haska was deeply in love with Gul Khan and she would go on talking to him until someone called her.

She reminded him of the beginning: the day, seven years before, when her mother had sent her sister to fetch Haska from a friend's house. "Haska! Baba has agreed to your marriage to Gul Khan, Babo wants you home." At the time she hadn't known whether to be happy or sad. Her friends began teasing her, so she left quickly and ran home.

Her sister Wreshmeena said, "If you look through the window, you'll see him. He's sitting right across from the window." She stood behind Haska, asking: "What do you think? Do you like him?"

Haska smiles now at Gul Khan's photograph. "You looked so handsome in your white kameez, with your black waistcoat," she says.

While they were looking through the window, her mother had come up behind the sisters, unseen. She shooed them away. "You are so naughty and shameless, go to your room! Imagine if someone came out and saw you here. Quick!"

As Haska was reminiscing with Gul Khan's portrait, Wranga came in and brought her abruptly back to the present. "Moor Jani! Moor Jani! My uncle has brought biscuits but he won't give me one."

"Why not?"

"He said, 'I brought these for my own children. You go

and ask your widowed mother for some.' Moor Jani, what is a widow?"

Haska shivered. "When you grow up and go to school, you will find out."

"Will my grandfather allow me?"

"Why not? Your father wanted you to go to school. When you turn six, I will make your wish come true."

Haska got up to avoid any more questions Wranga might ask that she couldn't answer. As she was walking across to the kitchen, her brother-in-law called her into the yard.

"Haska! Where are you going? Come here, you need to hear this."

Haska tugged at her scarf until it hid half her face and took her place with the other family members gathered in the yard. She was relieved to see that her mother had also come. Her husband's brother began to speak.

"All present here please listen carefully. If Haska won't marry me, I will not pay her children's expenses."

Haska was stunned. "Lalla! Who said that I am getting married? It hasn't even been four months since Jamal's father died. You know the iddat is not over."

"Enough! Enough! I know you want to remarry. All the men in the village are waiting to see who you will marry. If you don't want to marry, then why does every man care so much who you will marry? Today you hear it clearly: Haska will only marry me. I am not so dishonourable that you should marry someone else while I am here."

His mother added her voice to conclude the conversation. "Of course, son! This is our culture – a widow should marry her husband's brother. Haska is still young and she doesn't have anyone to feed her and her children. She can't live the rest of her life alone. When the time is right and the iddat is over, we will do the nikah."

Haska held her scarf across her face but her voice rose. "Adey, what are you saying? Lalla, what are you saying? I am not going to marry again."

"What did I tell you?" Her brother-in-law gave her a dirty look and left the yard.

Haska's parents-in-law also walked away, shaking their heads with concern. Her mother whispered to her: "My daughter, don't play with your life, this is our custom. Look at your neighbour: she married her brother-in-law after her husband died. She is happy."

Haska ran to her room. She took Gul Khan's portrait down and held it close. Then she leaned it against the mattress that was folded in one corner. Jamal followed her into the room. "Moor Jani, I heard what my uncle said. If you don't marry him, who will feed us?"

"Come and sit beside me, my blessed son. God will feed us. We are not supposed to think about it. Allah will give us what is in our destiny."

"There won't be any more biscuits?" asked Wranga, who had been watching from the doorway.

Haska tried to laugh. "God willing, we will eat biscuits.

But not today, another day." Haska looked at her daughter's drooping head. "I will bake some for you soon."

A little later, Haska was walking towards the kitchen when she heard something that made her look out into the yard. Wranga was sitting in front of a large basin next to a pile of dirty laundry. She was trying to wash the clothes with her tiny hands. Haska rushed over to her.

"My daughter, my daughter, what are you doing? Where did these clothes come from?"

"Zainub, my uncle's wife, said that if I wash these she will give me and Jamal an egg each."

Haska reached for her daughter's arm and pulled her up. As she was drying Wranga's little hands she saw that the hot water had turned them red. Her clothes were soaking too. Haska made an effort to hide her tears from Wranga. She said, brightly: "Go. Change your clothes and play. I will prepare something for you."

Haska found her sister-in-law Zainab feeding her children in the kitchen. Without saying a word, Haska went to the cupboard and picked up two eggs.

But a hand reached out for the eggs and a voice said: "Did you ask permission to take those? My husband has spent money on those eggs and you may not have them."

"My wrendar, my sister-in-law, my children have not eaten since morning and now the sun is setting. I'm not going to be eating the eggs myself, I am cooking them for the children.

Wranga was even washing clothes in order to eat; her little hands were scalded. How could you ask her to do such a thing?"

"I did the right thing. Let her learn the household chores. She will be getting married and going to someone else's home. She must not bring shame on us."

"God forbid. She is so little that, when she eats, she gets food on everything. It will be a long time before she is married."

"Go away. There is no egg for her. God knows what he wants from you. You brought misfortune to your own husband and now you want to impose yourself on my family."

The commotion brought the older women to the kitchen. Haska raised her voice.

"I won't marry your husband, how many times do you want me to say it?"

"That won't change his mind. You don't behave like a widow. You are full of charms and laughter, you go around like a single girl. No wonder men are interested in you. You should watch your behaviour: every day we hear you laughing."

"Zainab Jan, I laugh with my children."

"Whoever you laugh with, you have charmed my husband."

Haska said no more. She walked towards the well in the yard. Her mother and mother-in-law called after her: "Wait! Wait!"

Haska lowered her head into the well. Her mother was quickly at her side, pulling on her arm.

"What are you doing, girl?"

Haska didn't answer. She drew the bucket of water from the well and threw cold water on her face. Then she went to get two cups and filled them with water from the bucket. She called Jamal and Wranga and instructed Jamal to ask the neighbour for bread.

Jamal did as he was told. Haska took both her children to her room and broke the bread in two. She gave one piece to Jamal and one to Wranga and put the glasses of water down in front of them. Jamal didn't say anything but Wranga opened her tiny mouth to complain. "Moor Jani, you didn't cook an egg."

Haska was upset. "Be quiet and eat what's here. Or go to sleep." Wranga's mouth turned down at the corners. She ate a bite of the bread and drank a sip of water and soon fell asleep against the wall. Jamal tried hard to swallow.

The door opened slowly. Haska looked up and saw her mother, who came and sat beside her on the ground. She held Haska's hand in hers and spoke calmly.

"My girl, why are you behaving like this? Why do you want to spend your life in misery, allowing people to gossip about you? Your sister-in-law is badmouthing you and so is your brother-in-law. But he's alright – marry him. Your children will have a father and people will stop blaming you for things."

Jamal got a blanket and lay down. He covered his face with the blanket but he couldn't sleep, he was listening too carefully to the conversation.

Haska tried to explain. "I don't want a stepfather for my children. I don't want to be unfaithful to Jamal's father. I am happy to be called widow but not anybody else's wife."

"Do you want to spend the rest of your life alone?"

"I am not alone, I have my children.' Haska looked at her sleeping children and sighed. "I will work."

"You are illiterate – how can you work?"

"I don't know but I will find work – any work – and earn money."

"Haska, no woman in our family has ever worked. And your in-laws – what will you do?"

Haska didn't want to prolong the conversation so she said, "I have such a bad headache. I want to sleep. You stay here and go to sleep too, Babo."

She really did have a terrible headache, so she picked up a scarf and wrapped it around her head. Suddenly her eye was caught by a knot at one end of the scarf. There was a small round weight at the end. Haska untied the knot and found money inside that she had forgotten – from the night Gul Khan gave her money to keep safe while he returned to his shift at the pharmacy. Haska shot her husband's portrait a grateful look, and began counting the money. It would cover a month's expenses but she needed to do better than that.

Before dawn, Haska woke her mother, showed her the money and explained her plan to make biscuits. "Then you can take them to Nader-Uncle's shop next door, and see if he can sell them."

"But who will buy the biscuits you bake at home?"

"I can't think of anything else, Babo. Will you help me? Let's try it once and trust in God!"

When her mother saw how determined she was, she took the money Haska was holding out.

"Alright, but where I am going to find the ingredients?"

"Ask the neighbours while everyone else is asleep."

At four in the morning, her mother went next door. The neighbour opened the door to her and gave her the flour, oil, eggs and cardamom she wanted. Haska's mother paid her for them and returned to Haska.

Haska had already started the fire in the oven. She baked the biscuits before morning prayers and gave them to her mother, saying: "Tell Nader-Uncle that for as many biscuits as he manages to sell, I will share the profit fifty–fifty."

When she went to the shop, Haska's mother told him of her daughter's troubles and that she was badly in need of money. "Could you just keep the biscuits on your counter and see if anyone buys them?"

The shopkeeper relented. "Sure, leave them here and come back in the evening. We'll talk then."

Back at the house, Haska's brother-in-law was badgering her again.

"So, how long do you plan to go hungry? How will you

survive? If you won't have mercy on yourself, think of your children, they are hungry too." He said to Wranga, "If your mother agrees to what I say, I will give you breakfast right away."

Haska's mother-in-law said, "Son, please don't do this. They are little, they will suffer."

All day, Haska was anxious, rubbing her hands together and walking from one end of the yard to the other. She knew her mother would stop at Nader-Uncle's shop on her way back that evening. Haska waited nervously, and when she heard her mother return, she rushed to meet her at the door.

Haska's mother smiled at her daughter's worried face. "Please breathe, my child. Nader-Uncle sold all the biscuits. Here is your money."

"So much? There are a thousand afghanis here."

"He said he'd start taking his share of the profit next time. He said you should definitely keep baking them – everyone loved the home-made biscuits."

Haska's mother-in-law asked what the excitement was about.

"Adey, I have found a way to pay for my children's expenses, so I don't have to marry Lalla." She explained everything to the matriarch of the family. Her brother-in-law stood by listening. When he realised what she was saying, he said with fury:

"Our reputation was the only thing we had, now you have ruined that. You will bring shame on us if you go and talk with shopkeepers. Adey, tell her."

His mother replied impatiently: "If she doesn't want to marry you, why are you forcing her? No one will be happy in a marriage like that. If she bakes the biscuits at home and Jamal takes them to the shop, your reputation will not be hurt."

Haska's brother-in-law stood still for a second, stunned by his mother's ruling. Then he stormed off. "I won't have anything more to do with her. She is dead to me. Once a woman starts to work outside the home, you can no longer count on her."

Haska smiled.

PLEASE TURN THE AIR CONDITIONING ON, SIR

Maryam Mahjoba

*Translated from the Dari by Parwana Fayyaz
and Dr Zubair Popalzai*

If he says this out loud, everyone immediately around him will complain. Or they will mock him, given how cold the weather is at this time of year, happy that space is tight in the car and they have to sit close to one another. As the number of vehicles grows and the traffic gets worse, his sweat increases, and a warmth spreads from behind his neck over his whole body. When a bigger truck, full of bricks, stops beside their car, his body clenches. *If that truck is full of gas and petrol . . .* he grips the handle on the roof more tightly and turns his face to the person sitting next to him, but without any smile to offset his fear, his anger and his distress. So that no one will fight or make a scene, so they will not ask what they have done wrong to deserve such a look, he pretends that he wants to look at the shops or vehicles on their side. As he warms up, his cologne permeates the packed space inside the car and mixes with the smell of smoke and petrol and dust.

There is no escaping. When he looks beyond the window to his left, there is a loaded trailer. To his right sits a person and another person after that. When he looks past them, through the window, the vehicles are also full of people and they are moving slowly, slowly, one after another. Beyond them, there are grocery stores whose interiors are full of rice and oil, and whose exteriors are piled with crates of yellow and red apples, pomegranates and oranges. Their colours spread warmth. The smoke of kebabs slowly wafts upwards from a restaurant and disperses. On the floor above it is a café, its sign darkened by the smoke.

Slowly the Silo comes into view. The Silo building is so tall that it blocks out the silhouette of the mountains. There are two things no one has seen: no one has seen the Silo painted any colours other than yellow and white, nor has anyone seen the daily arrival and departure of its bread-makers. Although Hamed has been taking this route for the past eighteen years, he has never met or seen a single person who works at the Silo. Upset by this, he breathes deeply. The pavement is full of people. People with flesh and skin and veins and blood. People full of joy and sadness and wishes and God.

Oof, people – bags full of blood with green veins and black hair; with eyes that are black and white, green and white, and, occasionally, blue and white. People full of sorrow and depression, with hearts that are blackened by the world. People full of hope and joy from a few pieces of numbered paper, thanking God that life is still good.

Outside the vehicle, steam comes out of the mouths of the men and young children selling souvenirs in the streets. Thanks to the cold weather, it is as if everyone in the city is smoking a cigarette. This is the crowd who might at this moment, or a few moments later, explode with Hamed. With their veins full of blood and their skulls full of brains and nerves, they might disappear. Then he remembers the piece of cheese he left in the fridge for the following morning.

Will it stay there until tomorrow morning and forever more? Tomorrow morning will not come. Tomorrow morning – when I would have eaten that piece of cheese with sweet tea – will never come.

For these twenty-eight days he has gone to the office and come back. In two days, he will get his pay. *Two days from today.* Hamed speculates. For no reason at all, except for utter stupidity and ignorance, on this road, inside this vehicle, his veins full of blood may be torn apart. In two days' time, his pay will be transferred to the bank.

He checks one pocket, then the other, but there is no handkerchief. He puts his hand inside the pocket of his jacket and pulls out a light-turquoise handkerchief – on one corner of which is a pear embroidered in pink – and cleans the sweat from his forehead and neck. The handkerchief smells of cologne, the one he bought for three thousand afghanis from the Gulbahar Centre. The bottle is small but still full of cologne, like the people who are full of blood and wishes. It is too much . . . It isn't only the thought of death and being unexpectedly broken into pieces. What if, after this, his son becomes a gum seller or an addict, or if his daughter has to beg . . .

Oh God, I seek refuge in you, but all these orphans and beggars haven't fallen from the sky. They have been left behind. Left behind by people – half of whose blood seeped into the ground in the street while water washed the other half away; people buried, unwashed, as martyrs in the most crowded graveyard.

The sky is blue and clear and there is a gentle breeze. It is one of those days when the winter sun is gorgeous and you don't want even to think of death. The alley near the school is crowded for a cold day. Little girls and big girls, with their white chadors and coloured jackets that cover half the blackness of their shirts, crowd around the man selling candyfloss. Those who had eaten it first have pink-coloured lips and tongues. The memory of childhood turns to water in people's hearts, just like that sweet pink cotton wool in their mouths. Mothers take the hands of their small boys and pull them into the school. The car now stops at the school lane. As the north wind blows onto Hamed's body and dries his sweat, his phone rings.

"Hello, Hamed, are you OK?"

"Hello, yes, I got here fine!"

"There's been an explosion on Pul-e Charkhi Road. I called to check on you. Thankfully, you have got there."

"Pul-e Charkhi was not on my way, but thanks."

"Bye."

"Bye."

He goes into the school. His secretary, Kaka Kheir Mamad, runs towards him.

"Good morning, Mr Headmaster. Come, someone has been bothering me. He has been waiting for you since early morning. Mr Headmaster, these girls want to transfer to another school. Their father has brought the papers."

Hamed doesn't think it necessary to ask, "Are they not content here?"

Hamed knows that in government schools one doesn't ask those kinds of questions. It is completely against the pride and honour of these hallowed places. It is only the private schools that put themselves at the feet of their students. He himself understands that no one makes their journey to school longer because of the quality of their studies. It's possible that their father, like others from this area, has migrated to another place.

He looks at the document. Yes! Rabia Balkhi – so they have moved to Kart-e-Say or Kart-e-Char. He is now curious whether they got the house with a mortgage or if they rented. He can't imagine that the girls' father, with his shabby appearance, bought a house.

Kaka Kheir Mamad brings tea and chocolate that one of the students had brought in the day before as his graduation sweet. Hamed recalls that its wrapper was red and inside was chocolate mixed with nuts. It is now lunchtime. The smell of fried onions rushes in with every opening and closing of his office door. Hunger makes Hamed's mouth water and he asks his secretary, "Kaka Kheir Mamad, what are we having for lunch?" And Kaka Kheir Mamad answers, "What do the poor have for lunch, Mr Headmaster? Potato curry." Headmaster Hamed approves the transfer documents and hands them back.

When Kaka Kheir Mamad goes away, he is alone. During his tea break he suddenly feels crowded and restless again. Today his heart and mind won't rest on anything. The tea doesn't taste the same as usual. Why? It is as if demons are chasing him, and even though they are hidden from him now, Hamed can sense them. As he remembers his sister's call, fear runs through his heart and body. Why did his sister call him so randomly and ask how he was when she knew that the explosion wasn't on his route? Her asking gives him a bad feeling. What if today, on his way home, he gets caught up in a suicide attack and that becomes the last time that his sister will have heard his voice? Don't let it be that his sister has sensed that his death will come soon. He feels intensely low, his whole being tangled like a knot. He swallows, takes a deep breath. If he were a smoker, he would definitely smoke a cigarette.

He prays to God for strength as he gets up from behind the table and walks to the yard. The sun is high in the sky, warm and gentle. Hamed sits on a bench. The air is fresh and worth breathing. He moves bits of gravel around with his feet and doesn't realise at all that he is playing with the little stones. Yes, his heart and his attention are on the other side of the city, with the people who died today. Who are they to him and had they known that they would die today?

Had someone told them:

Hello, this morning at 8.23 a.m. you will die. Next to you is a vehicle full of explosives. We still don't know what kind of explosives but we know it will explode. It will suddenly burst into flames and you will be consumed by the flames.

If so, the people would have replied:

If it catches fire, let it catch fire, we will die anyway; your information is not that useful. It would have been better if you had said that today the weather will be cloudy, or that it will rain at 8.23 a.m. Death is certain and we are not afraid of it, but we do fear that our children will be orphans.

Hamed raises his head and looks around him at the dry, leafless trees and the empty courtyard of the school. It is a space he has seen again and again over many years, but it has never seen him so remorseful. He gets up and looks at his watch: it shows it is ten past two in the afternoon. Every day, he goes home from school at two-thirty, so why does he want to go now? What game is he caught in? Who wants to ensnare him? Or is it a mysterious positive force prompting him to leave at this hour? Should he go or not? Afterwards, they will say:

Hamed left school at two-thirty every day, but on the day he died he left at ten past two, dammit!

AFTERWORD

Lucy Hannah

There is an important section missing from this anthology. It's called About the Writers, and I wish it were here. The situation in Afghanistan at the time of writing means that profiles of the eighteen women whose stories feature here cannot, for now, be printed. We hope that future editions will be able to tell you more, and that the collection will also be published in Afghanistan – in Pashto and Dari – when it is safe to do so.

The absence of About the Writers says something of the difficult birth of this collection. *My Pen Is the Wing of a Bird* is the culmination of two years' work; of an intensive editorial process that worked across three languages, several countries and many time zones. It was a mix of hard labour, creative relationships and the best and worst of technology.

A dramatic punctuation point came in the summer of 2021.

The writers were working on their pieces for this anthology, when their creative process, and their lives more broadly, were thrown into question by the Taliban takeover, and the fall of Kabul. As the world watched the devastating scenes at Kabul airport and elsewhere in the country, our focus shifted swiftly from creativity to safety, working to support those writers who wanted to leave, and those who wished to – or had to – remain.

These eighteen women looked to each other for reassurance. They shared how they couldn't sleep, how they had dyed their clothes black, how they had soaked away the ink from pages of writing that was now a risk to possess as hard copy. Some took to the streets; others went into hiding; and six crossed borders and are now living in Germany, Italy, Iran, Sweden, Tajikistan and the USA. They, and the writers still in Afghanistan, all continued to write.

At the time, someone asked me: "Why would people carry on writing at a time like this?" And the answer is that, if you are a writer, that is what you do. Stories help us make sense of our world, particularly in the face of uncertainty and fear. As one of the writers said: "All we can do is give each other moral support. Sharing our writing is one way of doing that. War won't take our creativity away."

The writers in *My Pen Is the Wing of a Bird* came together through Untold's Write Afghanistan project, which started following conversations in Kabul with women scriptwriters on Afghanistan's long-running radio soap opera *New Home*,

New Life. They were frustrated by the lack of opportunity to publish their prose writing, and by the challenges of developing an internal market for their work. One had published short stories online, in Pashto and Dari, but she said: "I have never come across a local publisher willing to publish a book without asking for money from the author. And it's impossible to find a foreign publisher who wants to read books about anything except the war."

Short stories lend themselves to fractured, pressured environments. It makes sense that a form which contains complexity, beauty and truth in so few words, on such small canvases, feels easier to produce than something longer. Writing at length requires peace of mind, space, concentration and, crucially, the knowledge that if your work is strong enough, there is a well-developed local creative industry that has the enthusiasm and the resources to find you a readership.

In 2019, Untold put out an open call across Afghanistan, inviting women writers to submit short fiction in Dari and Pashto. Around one hundred submissions came in from all the major cities, along with a few from more rural provinces. Of those writers, one, who has two stories included here, was inspired by the opportunity to write several new pieces. But it was her older sister who submitted them to the call, because the writer felt she was too inexperienced for her work to be taken seriously. She had never shared her writing, had never edited or rewritten a story, and had not been able to attend any of the rare writers' meetings in the capital.

A second open call, in early 2021, focused on the more isolated parts of the country. The word was spread on social media, via radio broadcasts, and on posters in the smaller towns and villages. This time, two hundred writers in twenty provinces sent in work from internet cafés, home computers and mobile phones. One of the stories in this collection was written by hand, photographed and sent via WhatsApp messages through a chain of people before reaching Untold.

The stories were set in the home, at work, in the future and long ago. They touched on universal themes of family, friendship, love and betrayal. Fiction, yes, but often inspired by real-life events. It was crucial to Write Afghanistan that the writers tell the stories they wanted to write, without any prescribed themes or narratives thrust upon them.

Literary translation has been at the heart of Write Afghanistan. A team of Afghan readers selected writers from the open calls to collaborate with international editors and translators. These working relationships developed via WhatsApp, Zoom, SMS, email – whatever was needed for safety and for accessibility. The process continued in spite of the pandemic (Afghanistan has known the word "lockdown" since long before Covid-19) with the editors, translators and writers discussing drafts of stories in one language, for readers in another. Words were lost and found. The internet went down. Power failed and lights would cut out, but the urge to write was always undimmed.

One of the many joys of reading is that the literature of

a world far from our own has the potential to alter how we see ourselves. For writers lucky enough to live in a place with a healthy publishing infrastructure, their imagined worlds have the chance to reach and engage readers far beyond their country's borders. For many of the writers in this anthology, it has been a different story. *My Pen Is the Wing of a Bird* is just a small sample of these writers' work; they continue to write fiction in their own languages, ready for readers both at home and across the globe.

The contributors agreed that this book should not say anything about the writers, and several have chosen to use a pen name. But the majority have insisted on using their real names because they are adamant that they be read and their voices heard. I'd like to leave the last word to Maryam Mahjoba, one of the writers in this anthology, who expresses this best, when she says:

We see someone from afar and think thoughts about their behaviours and habits. Sometimes we get angry and ask ourselves: why do they do such things? Why did they make such a decision? Perhaps, drawing from the circumstances of our own lives, we offer them solutions.

If we talk to the person we see from afar and begin to unwrap their stories about childhood and youth and dreams, we might think differently. A woman in Europe or America wears high heels, and a woman in Afghanistan wears them too. But are our feet really in the same shoes?

I do not speak any language other than my mother tongue, and I can see how much I need to speak. One cannot love or have the right to hate without understanding and being understood. How do we know anything about what it means to live amid another community or culture or religious practice?

We women, we are minorities. We want to be heard, listened to . . .

Yes, does anyone hear my voice?

Yes. Is there someone?

I am drowning. Help! Help!

What if we did not know the meaning of these words?

Nothing has the power to express our thoughts and feelings as words do. We can only enter the inner world of other humans by translating the words of a language into a language we are familiar with. For this reason, even God needs words and language to talk with humans. He called on humans: "Nuon. Oath to the pen and to what it writes." (Quran, Surah 68 Al-Qalam (the Pen), verse 1.)

If there was no translation from one language to another, would we be the same kind of humans that we are today? Would we have something called literature?

We must open this way and make it wider, to make our experiences of living become even deeper and more meaningful.

Afghanistan has never been heard or understood.

Who are these people? And what do they want? How did they endure forty-two years of war? To find the answers, we must talk about these questions. And we would like to share our words with you. Make our words familiar to you.

There is a story told by Maulana Balkhi, whom you may know as Rumi, in the *Masnavi*. A Persian, an Arab, a Turk and a Greek were travelling together, and they received a present of a dirhem. The Persian said he wished to buy "angur" with it, the Arab said he would buy "inab", while the Turk and the Greek were for buying "üzüm" and "astaphil", respectively. They argued as to which of them would get his way, until a wise man, who spoke all their languages, intervened. He explained that they all wanted grapes.

I also want grapes.

ACKNOWLEDGEMENTS

This project would not have been possible without the skills of Untold's Write Afghanistan team. Thank you to project manager Will Forrester for his unswerving commitment and to editors Sunila Galappatti and Jacob Ross for their insight and support. A special thanks to the project's cultural adviser, writer and editor, Zarghuna Kargar, for her belief in the importance of Afghan women's stories.

We are grateful to translators Alireza Abiz, Parwana Fayyaz, Shekiba Habib, Margo Munro Kerr and Dr Zubair Popalzai for their skills and patience. Thank you to interpreter and translator Dr Negeen Kargar, whose enthusiasm never waned, and we wish all the best to interpreter Pashtana Durrani. We are indebted to reader Kawoon Khamoosh. Also, thank you to Patrick Spaven for his evaluation skills.

This team could not have come together without the

continued support of Untold's partners: the British Council, in particular Dana MacLeod and Tamanna Faqirzada, and the Bagri Foundation. We are also incredibly grateful to: the Lund Trust, a charitable fund of Lisbet Rausing and Peter Baldwin, the Oak Foundation and the Rothschild Foundation, who supported the project at a key moment. We'd also like to thank Fondation Jan Michalski, the PF Charitable Trust and the Robert Gavron Charitable Trust for their generosity.

Thanks to King's College London and the Centre for Life Writing Research, where Clare Brant continues to champion our work. A special thank you to Ms Alison Blake CMG, former British Ambassador to Kabul, and Ambassador Yama Yari, for their interest in Write Afghanistan.

We are grateful to Prospero World, in particular Anna-Louisa Psarras, for adopting Untold as one of its chosen causes, and to all those who contributed to our emergency appeal fund in August 2021 – your generosity helped these writers to stay connected at a critical time.

Thank you to our volunteers: Judith Witting, for her keen eye on the figures, Caroline Banerjee, Lena Dias Martins, Phoebe Hamilton-Jones and Trà My Hickin.

Untold thanks all those who helped in various ways, including Clare Alexander, Antonia Byatt, Nicola Dahrendorf, Amelia Fitzalan-Howard, James Greenshields, Daniel Hahn, Dr Samay Hamed, Mary Hockaday, Rob Jago, Rabia Latif Khan, Penny Lawrence, Daniela Leykam, Nerissa Martin, Chelsea Pettit, Anne Phillipson, Homeira Qaderi, Sana Safi,

Shirazuddin Siddiqi, Murray Shanks and Janie Wilson for their wise counsel and expertise, and is hugely grateful to those who spread the word for Write Afghanistan: Emma Duncan, Matthew Fort, Marion Hume and Lou Stoppard.

We are grateful to Susan Harris and Samantha Schnee at *Words Without Borders*, who first published four of these stories. Also, to our project partner, Annika Reich at Weiter Schreiben, for publishing several writers from the Write Afghanistan project in Germany.

Thank you to our chair and co-director, Sarah Gardner, for her time and strategic thinking, and to co-director Bill Hicks for helping to establish Untold Narratives CIC.

A big thank you to Katharina Bielenberg, Robina Pelham Burn, Rose Green, Milly Reid and Lipfon Tang at MacLehose Press for taking the leap to bring these eighteen writers' stories from one part of the world to readers in another.

Finally, thank you to all the writers who so enthusiastically joined the Write Afghanistan project: we look forward to continuing our work together.